IN LOVE WITH A HEARTLESS MENACE 2

TAY MO'NAE

STAY UP TO DATE WITH TAY MO'NAE

Want to stay up to date with my work? Be the first to get sneak peeks, release dates, cover reveals, character updates, and more? Join my Facebook reading group: Tay's Book Baes and like my like page: Tay Mo'Nae.
Make sure you check my website out for updates as well: Taymonaewrites.com
Also, join my **mailing list** for exclusive first by texting **AuthorTay** to **33777**

*These H*es Doin' Too Much (SA)*

*These H*es Actin' Up (SA)*

Can't Help but Love You (SA)

Stroking The Flame Within Her Heart (Novella)

DISCLAIMER

This is a **RERELEASE**. No new material has been added.

CHAPTER 1

RENEE

My heart pounded like drums as it beat loudly.

Today was the day I dreaded. I didn't want to deal with anyone, especially not the person standing in front of me right now.

A blank stare was on my face as Matt stood on my front steps.

"I don't get why you're here," I said dryly.

"Why wouldn't I be here? Today our baby was supposed to be born." My chest ached from hearing the words out loud.

"I still don't understand why you're here," my voice remained emotionless.

"Come on, Renee. You shut me out and wouldn't let me be there for you. Today is hard for the both of us." My stomach turned.

The sadness that was just present quickly diminished and was replaced with anger.

"Why the hell would I let you be there for me. You're the reason why I'm not celebrating the birth of my child! I don't want shit from you but for you to leave me alone!" Tears ran down my cheek as my chest rose and fell quickly.

"I told you I was sorry about that, baby. I didn't know Jada was going to come and fight you. I regret that shit!"

"And I regret meeting you! Leave me alone and don't bother me again!" I yelled and slammed my door shut.

I leaned back on my door and allowed my head to drop. Tears continued to run down my face. I squeezed my eyes shut and placed my hands on my stomach.

The fact that I was supposed to be bringing my baby into the world today was heavy on my heart. The nerve of Matt coming over here trying to console me. That only caused my hatred for him to grow deeper.

I pushed myself off the door and headed back to my room. I had been laying around all day trying to block out the world, but Matt was persistent when he came knocking on my door.

Laying back on my pillow, I saw my phone light up. I reached over and saw that Brady had reached out to me again.

I swallowed hard. Tears continued to cloud my vision as I stared at his name. I felt bad for ignoring him, but I wasn't in the right mind to deal with him right now.

Licking my dry lips, I opened his message and vaguely smiled through my tears. Taking a deep breath, I decided I needed a break from everyone, including Brady.

I LAID in the dark under my covers on my tear-drenched pillow. I was gripping my sonogram close to me with my eyes closed as I wept.

I thought my mood would have improved as the day went on, but after Matt left, it only seemed to get worse.

Brady never did reply to my text message and it kind of stung, but I understood. He was a good guy, but right now I know I was no good for him.

I closed my eyes and clenched the sonogram closer.

My eyes popped open when someone started knocking on my door. I stayed where I was at, hoping the person would go away, but they wouldn't let up. They began ringing my doorbell and I groaned.

Snatching the covers from over my head, I jumped out of bed and stormed to the front of my house.

I swear if this Matt again, I was fighting his ass.

I got to the door and snatched it open, ready to go off on whoever was on the other side.

My voice got caught as I stared into Brady's squinted eyes. He didn't speak, only looked me over. When he focused on my face, the scowl on his face deepened.

"What are you doing here?" I finally asked.

Instead of answering me right away, he barged into my house, pushing past me. I closed my eyes and released a deep breath before closing the door.

"Look, Brady-"

"What the fuck was up with that text Renee?" he cut me off and asked.

I took a minute to take in his handsome face. Even staring at me with a frown on his face, he was still good looking.

"Brady look, I just don't think now is a good time for us to be together," I said quietly, looking down at the ground.

"That shit don't work for me. We were just good. What changed?"

I brought the sonogram picture that was still in my hand to the front of me and looked down at it. The tears that had stopped for the moment suddenly started back. My shoulders began to shake, and I closed my eyes.

"Baby." Brady stepped closer to me. "What's wrong?"

He reached out and went to grab the sonogram picture, but I

snatched it back. "Please, Brady, just go!" This time my voice was a little louder.

"If I walk out that door. I'm not coming back, Renee."

I brought my eyes to meet his and I could tell he was serious. Even though I didn't want that, I felt like that was best at the moment.

Brady and I stared at each other until he nodded and went to step around me. I quickly grabbed his wrist, instantly feeling my heart ache even more as he attempted to leave.

"Today was my due date," I confessed.

He turned to face me, and now a sympathetic look was on his face. He didn't speak any words, only grabbed me and pulled me into him. His arms tightened around me and he allowed me to cry into his chest.

"I'm sorry," he whispered, rubbing my back.

"I just have so many emotions running through me right now." Brady kissed the top of my head, and the sound of his heartbeat surprisingly started to calm me. Being in his arms right now gave me a sense of relief.

"I don't want you to leave me," I said into his chest.

"I'm not going anywhere." He bent down and kissed me.

I sighed against his lips feeling tension slowly leave my body.

Brady pulled away from me and grabbed my hand, leading me back into my bedroom.

When we got into my room, he stripped down to his boxers and got in bed behind me. His arms wrapped around me, and he pulled me close to him.

"You don't have to worry about going through anything alone again," he said into the back of my head.

I melted into my chest and placed my hands over his.

Being in Brady's arms provided a certain calmness for me. My tears had stopped finally, and my body relaxed while wrapped in his.

CHAPTER 2

NAUDIA

THE FOOD IN MY HAND DROPPED AS MY BLOOD BOILED. I COULD feel my body growing hot as I stared at the scene in front of me.

Angrily, I started clapping at the performance I was currently watching.

Tariq's attention went from sucking on Chyna's breast over to me. "Fuck!" he yelled, and his body jerked.

My eyes went to Chyna's. She was sitting on Tariq staring at me with a smirk on her face. "Naudia, what the fuck!" Tariq said, throwing Chyna off him.

"Seriously, Tariq!" she yelled, but he ignored her.

My eyes went to his dick, and I noticed not only was he not wearing a condom, but it had cum leaking from it.

My hands clenched on the side of me. I could feel myself about to go off and was trying not to.

The fact that Tariq had made it seem like he was going to break things off with Chyna so we could make it work, only for me to walk in on the two of them fucking, hurt. It made my chest burn.

"I thought you were leaving her?" I finally said, taking my eyes off his dick and looking him in the eye.

"Leaving me? What the hell is she talking about, Tariq?" Chyna asked him, stepping near him.

He ignored her just like the first time.

He quickly put his dick away and went to take a step towards me, but I stepped back. He squinted his eyes and glared at me.

"Why the fuck do you keep popping up over here anyway? You need to check this bitch," Chyna said, facing Tariq. His eyes never left mine though. I could see the conflict in his face.

"Call me another one," I told her.

Chyna turned towards me. "Why are you still here bitch? Whatever little crush your little hoe ass has on my nigga needs to go away!"

That caused me to snap, and I charged at her hitting her soon as I got close enough. That seemed to snap Tariq out of his trance. He quickly snatched me up by my waist as Chyna and I started going at it. He gripped my waist tightly and turned so that he was blocking Chyna from hitting me.

"Get the fuck off me!" I yelled, trying to break free. I wanted to cry being in his arms right now, but I refused to show any weakness in front of Chyna's ass.

"Hit me again and Ima fuck you up!" he told her.

"Here you go defending this young hoe again! I'm your fucking girlfriend, Tariq. Kick this bitch out!" I could hear the frustration in her voice.

"That should tell you something bitch!" I yelled, trying to break free again.

"I don't have time for this shit. Chyna, I'll holla at you later," he finally told her.

"What! No, I'm not leaving. Kick her out!"

"Chyna, I said I'll holla at you later," his voice was stern.

She mumbled something under her breath and looked at me, causing me to smile at her. Chyna bit down on her bottom lip and blew out a deep breath before storming towards the door.

Once he heard the door closed, Tariq loosened his grip on me. I broke free from him and turned around, pushing him.

"Are you fucking serious, Tariq!" I yelled.

"Keep your fucking hands to yourself, Naudia!"

"Why were you fucking her! I thought you told me you were going to leave her!" I sniffed back the tears that were threatening to fall. Seeing Tariq fuck another girl made me sick. It caused something inside of me to break. We weren't official, but we had made plans to get there.

I promised to stop sleeping around because we were supposed to be working towards being together.

"Naudia, I called her over to break up with her," he started.

"So how did your dick end up in her!" I threw my hands up and my voice elevated.

"Lower your damn voice."

"No, you talked all this shit about how I should be with a nigga that respected me, and I deserved this and that, and look what you did."

"You knew I had a fucking girl, Naudia! Me and you aren't together."

"So the fuck what! You made it seem like we were going to be." I pulled on the end of one of the braids in my hair.

Tariq was bringing out feelings in me I hadn't felt before. Feelings that I never wanted to experience. Feelings that I purposely avoided.

Tariq tugged on his beard and shook his head. "Look, Naudia, me and Chyna were together for two years. It isn't easy to just leave someone after all that time."

My eyes narrowed. I tapped my foot and quickly wiped my eyes before tears could fall.

"This is why I never tried to take any of you niggas serious." I was over this situation. If Tariq wanted to stay with Chyna, then there was no point in me staying here arguing with him. In the end, I was the only one who was being hurt.

Just when I was about to turn to leave, Tariq called my name. I paused and cut my eyes at him.

"I meant what I said about wanting to be with you and making this work. Today I brought Chyna here to break up with her. I didn't bring her here to fuck her. Shit just kind of happened."

I slowly nodded. Tariq stepped up to me and I took a step back. He stopped and raised his eyebrow.

I didn't want him close to me. Usually, being near Tariq would give me a bubbly feeling, but I was too angry right now. It hurt my feelings knowing that we didn't even get a chance to be together before Tariq fucked up.

"I'm just going to go, Tariq," I told him. There was no point in me still being here. He showed me what was up, and I was going to have to accept it.

"Naudia, just chill the fuck out, damn. You act like I didn't just walk in on you and another nigga."

"You walked in on him leaving. At the time, me and you didn't agree to work towards being together either! You told me I needed to get my shit together and I been doing that. I was serious when I said I liked you, Tariq. You made me feel like I mattered, like I deserved more. The way you handled me showed me that you really did care about me."

"And nothing has changed, Naudia."

"It's all changed. I won't let you go between Chyna and me. I'm not going to share you with that bitch!"

Tariq chewed on the inside of his cheek. "I'm not trying to go between you two. I know who I want-"

"Obviously not because I just walked in on you fucking her!" My head started to hurt from yelling.

This was crazy. Tariq wasn't even my boyfriend and I'm here arguing with him.

Tariq stepped closer to me, and this time I didn't move. He grabbed me and pulled me into him. I rested my forehead on his chest and inhaled, frowning upwards.

"Her perfume is on you," I said quietly.

Tariq pulled me away and stared down at me. "I shouldn't have fucked her, especially after being hard on you like I was. That was my fuck up, but I do want to try with you, Naudia. The connection we have is something I never had with anyone before. I'll make this right."

I shook my head. "No, Tariq. I told you I wasn't going to let you treat me any kind of way. I'm not going to end up like my mom. You can stay with your girlfriend, and I'll go back to doing me."

Tariq let me go. "So what, you about to go back to fucking any nigga that smiles at you?"

I smirked. "If I want to." I shrugged.

Tariq chuckled and nodded his head. "Then have fun." He stepped back.

I stared at him curiously. "That's it?"

"I don't know what you expected me to say. You're grown, right? If that's what you want to do, then who am I to stop you?"

His noncaring attitude had only pissed me off even more. "I'm glad we both agree on something then."

I didn't give him a chance to say anything back to me. I turned and started towards his door. A part of me wanted him to stop me again, but he didn't. I looked over my shoulder and he was staring at me with his arms crossed.

Licking my lips, I turned back around and walked out his door.

Tariq was just like the guys he kept warning me about. The guys he kept telling me didn't give a fuck about me. I was just happy he showed me that now and not when I became fully invested.

CHAPTER 3
LUCAS

MY EYE TWITCHED AS I STARED BETWEEN TRINITY AND TREVOR. While Trevor looked unbothered by my question, Trinity looked like she was about to pass out.

"Baby-" she started, but I raised my hand to stop her.

"What the fuck is this nigga talking about, Tri?" I chewed on my bottom lip and narrowed my eyes.

"It was a mistake."

I closed my eyes and chuckled lowly. Shaking my head, I grabbed the back of my neck and squeezed it.

"I know you didn't fuck this nigga, Trinity." I opened my eyes back up and stared at her. She now had tears running down her face. Normally that would faze me, but this time it did nothing. It only infuriated me more.

"Lucas, man listen, that shit is old."

"Shut the fuck up! I wasn't talking to you," I sneered at him. "Did you fuck this nigga?" I asked Trinity again.

"I'm sorry," she whispered and dropped her head.

All the sense I had went out the window as I rushed Trevor tackling him to the ground. Trinity screamed as we went crashing into my table. I was quickly sending punches to his face. Trevor wasn't a slouch when it came to fighting, but he couldn't fuck with me and the anger I was feeling.

"Lucas please!" Trinity yelled behind me.

I ignored her and continued sending punches. "You fucked my girl?" I yelled.

Trevor groaned and threw his hands up. "Lucas, man," he struggled to get out.

Trinity grabbed my shoulders and I shrugged her off. She stumbled backwards and fell on her ass.

I stood up and sent my foot down on Trevor's face a few times. "Get the fuck out of my crib! Next time I see you, you better hope I don't have my piece on me," I growled.

I quickly turned to Trinity. She was still on the ground staring at me with fear in her eyes. I towered over her, staring at her disgusted. All this time, I thought I was the only one to ever be in her. I thought she was pure, a good girl, but she had me fooled.

"Get the fuck out," I told her.

"Lucas, please let me talk to you," she cried, standing up.

Her body, along with her voice, was shaking. "Trinity-"

"No, it was one time and a mistake. I was pissed because you kept cheating on me, and it just happened. I'm sorry," she cried.

I closed my eyes and Trevor mentioning the DNA test she had done on my daughter caused me to snap again. I quickly grabbed her neck and lifted her off the ground.

Trinity's eyes grew in size as she struggled to break loose. "If you weren't my daughter's mother, I would snap your fucking neck. You had me fooled thinking you were a good girl, but you're just like the rest of these hoes." Trinity started clawing at my hands and I finally let her go.

"My fucking daughter Trinity. My baby," my voice started to crack. "You didn't even make that nigga wrap it up."

Trinity was crying and holding her neck, gasping for air. "The condom broke," she struggled out.

I turned my mouth up at her. "I'll hit you up when I'm coming to get my daughter," I told her and looked behind me. While I was facing Trinity, snapping on her, I didn't even realize Trevor had taken my warning and left.

"Lucas, can we talk? I can explain," she begged.

I couldn't even look at her. "I'm cool on you. I don't want shit to do with you outside my daughter."

"You can't do that!" she yelled, stomping her foot. "I took you back every time you cheated, every time you lied. I made one mistake and you're just done! You can't do that," her cries grew louder.

"You shouldn't have. I don't want to be with you, Trinity. Me and you are a wrap. Take yo ass home or go find Trevor. I don't give a fuck to be honest." I crossed my arms and glared down at her.

She continued to cry in front of me. Her eyes begged me to forgive her, but I didn't feel sorry for her. Trinity had betrayed me. Not with some random nigga either. Trevor was someone I grew up with, my boy. She had me looking like a damn fool, having that nigga laugh at me knowing he fucked my bitch.

I saw how he was staring at her too. He wanted to fuck her again. That alone made me want to put one between his eyes.

Trinity finally saw I wasn't budging and nodded her head. "I know what I did was wrong, but I regret it. I never betrayed you, and we weren't even together when it happened."

Still, I gave her nothing but a blank stare.

Trinity turned and walked out of my door with her head hung.

Once she closed it behind her, I stepped towards the closest wall to me and sent my fist through it.

"Fuck!" I yelled.

Just knowing that Trinity let another nigga enter her caused my stomach to turn. Me wanting to make shit work with her wasn't even a thought to me anymore. Now all we had between us was our daughter. Trinity was free game from this point on.

CHAPTER 4

TRINITY

I CRIED ALL THE WAY TO MY HOUSE RECALLING THE WORDS LUCAS had just spoken to me. Sleeping with Trevor wasn't something I meant to happen. As soon as we were done, I knew I had fucked up and begged Trevor never to mention it to anyone.

I loved Lucas and knew if he ever found out what I did, he would be pissed and leave me. Trevor had taken advantage of me at a moment of weakness.

Lucas and I had been arguing for the past week over some girl that kept calling and texting his phone. He told me she was a nobody, but I knew better.

There was a house party going on the night I told Lucas I was done with him because I knew he was cheating on me. Naudia and Renee had convinced me to go because their fast asses wanted to go. They were only seventeen at the time and knew Lucas wouldn't allow them to come.

Even though I wasn't in the mood, I decided to get dressed and make sure I looked my best, knowing Lucas would be there.

When we got to the party, I instantly regretted coming. It was packed, and smoke filled the house along with loud music, but that wasn't the issue. The issue was Lucas was sitting in the corner surrounded by a few of his friends with the same bitch that had been hitting him up in his lap.

"I knew I shouldn't have come," I said, staring at Lucas and the girl.

Naudia looked over and she frowned.

"Girl, you got to toughen up," she snapped and stormed over to where her brother was before I could stop her. I looked over at Renee and she shrugged.

Renee grabbed my hand and pulled me behind Naudia.

"You're so fucking stupid, Lucas! Who is this?" Naudia yelled, mugging the girl.

"No, the real question is why is your young ass here," Lucas snapped.

Naudia ignored him and looked at the girl. "You know my brother has a girlfriend, right? All you are is some easy hoe."

"Obviously, she wasn't doing something right if he's here with me." The girl's eye fell on me.

"Aye shut the fuck up," Lucas snapped and looked at me.

"What's up, Tri!" He nodded towards me.

I started to get emotional. "You just couldn't wait, huh?" I finally asked him.

"Shit, you left me," he shrugged.

"Trinity, just give me the word and I'll beat this bitch up for you," Naudia told me.

I shook my head. "It's not even worth it. Your brother is a headache that I'm happy to get rid of." I turned and walked away.

I had made it a few steps before Lucas came up behind me grabbing me. "So it's like that?" he asked.

I snatched away from him. "Leave me alone, Lucas!"

"No, I'm not leaving you alone. You dumped me and then get mad when you see me with another bitch."

"We just broke up this morning, not even twenty-four hours

ago, and you're hugged up with another girl!" I tried not to, but Lucas always brought out so many emotions in me. It had been like this since I met him. Tears clouded my vision.

"Baby, she doesn't mean shit to me. I was just mad that you left me. I didn't do shit with her." He pulled me into him and hugged me.

"Lucas, are you for real!" The girl yelled behind us, instantly bringing me to my senses.

"Just leave me alone!" I spat and pushed him away from me.

I took off through the crowd of people into one of the bedrooms. I didn't want to party and be around anyone right now.

There was a knock on the door soon after I entered the room. "Lucas, go away!" I yelled.

The door opened and Trevor popped his head inside.

"You good?" he asked, walking into the room and shutting the door.

"I don't get why he does this to me," I cried, throwing my hands over my face.

"You're too pretty to be in here crying over a nigga," he said.

I looked up and noticed he had stepped closer to the bed I was sitting on.

Trevor looked me over and licked his lips. "I just wish he could love me like I love him." I dropped my head.

Trevor walked over to the bed and sat down next to me. He put his arm around my shoulder and pulled me into him. I closed my eyes and laid on his chest.

"Lucas is my nigga but he's dumb as fuck to leave a girl like you."

"A girl like me?" I whispered.

"You're beautiful, loyal, funny, and caring. You go hard for that nigga and he doesn't appreciate it. I tell him all the time he needs to do better."

I slowly lifted my head and looked at Trevor.

He was a good-looking guy. Caramel-colored skin, thick pink lips surrounded by a small goatee. Trevor always kept his hair cut low and lined up. He had light brown eyes that usually shined in the light. He was muscular and had a few tattoos scattered on his body.

"Trevor."

He grabbed my chin and lifted it, placing his lips on mine. I closed my eyes and allowed his tongue to invade my mouth.

"This isn't right," I said against his mouth. Trevor shifted his body and forced my body back. He was on top of me and began to kiss my neck.

"He hurt you, right?"

I nodded my head. "So let me heal you." He reached between my legs and rubbed on my pussy on the outside of my shorts.

I moaned softly and closed my eyes. My head went back, and my heartbeat quickened.

I knew this wasn't right. "Lucas will be mad," I whined.

Trevor kissed down my neck and lifted my shirt and bra up, taking my nipple in his mouth.

"He won't know. That nigga out there with that bitch for real."

I closed my eyes as my body heated up. "Just let me take care of you," he said against my skin.

After we were finished, my conscience quickly took over and I felt like shit. Just because Lucas had cheated on me didn't mean I needed to hook up with his friend. When I found out the condom broke, I started freaking out, but Trevor assured me that he pulled out in time.

The next week was my birthday and Lucas and I got back together. I felt guilty for my actions and took him back when he told me he was sorry and would change.

A month later, I found out I was pregnant, and panic sunk in. I prayed every day that my baby was Lucas's. I was going to tell him what happened, but I chickened out every time. He was so happy finding out I was having his baby that I couldn't bust his bubble.

When Lucia was a month old, I got her tested. She looked just like Naudia as a baby, but I had to be sure. Trevor kept making comments about it possibly being his baby and I couldn't have that over my head.

Thankfully, the test showed that Trevor wasn't the father. After that, he got into some trouble and left town. I was able to push the night with him aside and work on my family.

Now that my secret was out, I was lost on what to do. Even though I wanted to take a break from Lucas, I didn't want to give up on us. I loved him. I just wanted him to get his act together for me and our daughter. Seeing how disgusted he was when he looked at me made me feel dirty. I wish I never took it there with Trevor.

Now my family was ruined, and Lucas hated me.

———

"Sis, I thought you were over here dead." Naudia laughed, walking into my house.

I shut the door behind her but didn't say anything. I walked back into my living room and took the seat I was just previously occupying.

"Trinity, what's wrong?" Naudia sat next to me.

For the past two days, I had been in my head, not wanting to be bothered. My parents still had Lucia, and Lucas texted me telling me he would get her from their house. When I asked if we could talk, he didn't respond.

"My brother texted me and told me to come check on you. What's going on?"

I slowly took my eyes off the blank TV screen I been staring at all morning and looked at her.

"I fucked up," I confessed quietly.

"What did you do?"

I swallowed hard before revealing what happened with me and Trevor. Naudia's mouth dropped.

"Damn Trinity, I know Lucas flipped shit."

I nodded. "I thought he was going to kill me. In his face, I could see he wanted to. He was hurt and angry." I started crying. "I didn't mean for me and Trevor to happen. I had a moment of weakness."

That night had been playing over in my head since I left Lucas's house. I knew that it would eventually come and bite me in the ass; I just wished that Lucas would talk to me.

"Trinity, Ima keep it real with you; it was wrong for you to smash the homie, but I mean, you and Lucas weren't together. I remember that party and my brother was wrong. He can't be mad because you found comfort in someone else."

"It was his friend though."

"Girl, Trevor is fine as hell. I don't blame you."

"So you would've done the same thing?"

She scrunched her face up. "Hell no. I'm bold but Tariq would fuck me up if I did that shit," she laughed. "But hell, how I'm feeling right now got me tempted." Naudia suddenly began to frown.

"What happened?"

Naudia rolled her eyes and started examining her nails. "I walked in on Tariq fucking Chyna."

The way she said it was so calm, which wasn't like Naudia at all. Naudia was just like her brother, both hot heads ready to pop off whenever something happened they didn't like.

"What did you do?"

She looked at me and smiled. "Tried to beat that hoes ass, cursed him out, and left."

"That's it?"

She nodded. "Tariq knew why I didn't do relationships and why I just kept guys around to have sex. He told me he wanted me to change so we could be together, but he was still fucking Chyna instead of ending things like he said he would. That only confirmed things for me. I'm over it," she shrugged.

I stared at her curiously. Naudia was playing hard right now, but by the way she was clenching her jaw and squinting her eyes, I could see she was bothered by Tariq's actions. Naudia thought it was a crime to show any emotions, so she always kept her feelings bottled up.

"Anyway, I didn't come over here to talk about that. I want to know that you're okay?"

I shrugged. "I don't know. Even after everything, I still want to be with your brother. He's all I know. I just wish he would forgive me like I did him countless times."

"Trinity, Ima tell you the truth. You made it too easy for my brother. Even now, you're sitting here all sad and depressed while he's out living his life. I'm not saying it's not affecting him because I know it is, but he's not sitting in the house letting it stop his life. Show him that you don't need him. Lucas likes control. Stop giving him that over you."

I let Naudia's words sink in. I knew she wasn't lying. Me moving out was the first time I actually put some fire under Lucas. Instead of sitting around all depressed, I needed to show Lucas that with or without him, I was good.

"You're right. I need to get my shit together," I ran my hands through my untamed hair.

Naudia slapped her hands on my thigh and squeezed it. "Trust me, if Lucas sees that you're not affected by his actions, it'll make him mad and he'll be back. I'm rooting for you two, but I don't want you to let this stop your life."

I nodded. "Thanks, sis. I know that's your brother, but you're never biased."

"That's because I know my brother is an idiot and is wrong most of the time." I laughed.

Naudia stood up and stretched. "Okay, I'm going to go check on Renee next. I haven't talked to her in a few days besides a few texts."

I nodded. "Let me know if she's okay." I stood up and pulled Naudia in a hug.

"I know that everyone is always hard on you, but you're a great person, Naudia," I told her, letting her go.

She hugged me and laughed. "Thanks, sis. Now go take a shower." She pushed me away, making me laugh.

"Fuck what I just said, huh?" I shook my head.

Naudia smiled. "I'll call you later."

I nodded and followed behind her to the door.

What Naudia said made a lot of sense. Sadly, it was easier said than done. I wanted to do what she said and show I was unaffected by me and Lucas's current situation, but I knew it wouldn't be easy.

CHAPTER 5

NAUDIA

I knocked on Renee's door and waited for her to answer.

I knew she was here because her car was in the driveway and she hadn't been to class in the past few days.

Remembering I had a key to her place, I went into my purse to grab my keys when the door suddenly opened.

"Hoe, I thought I was going to have to call the damn cops to break the door down," I frowned at her.

"Sorry, I been dealing with a lot," she said quietly, moving to the side.

I walked into the house. "What's going on with you, Nae?" I asked, looking her over. I noticed how sad she looked. She didn't seem like her normal self; her energy was all off and gloomy.

"Aye Renee, I'm about to go meet up with the guys. Call me if you need me." Brady walked up to her and pulled her to his side, kissing her forehead.

"Okay," Renee told him.

He looked at me. "What's up, sis?" I stared at the two of them curiously.

"Hey."

Brady bent down and pecked Renee's lips before letting

her go.

Renee's door closed and I popped my hands on my hips. "Okay, so now I'm really lost. What's wrong?"

Renee took a deep breath. "My due date," was all she said.

My eyes widened and suddenly I felt like shit. "Friend!" I rushed her, throwing my arms around her. "I completely forgot. I'm sorry."

Renee hugged me back and I could hear her sniffling.

"It's okay. Brady was here helping me."

I let her go. I felt like shit. I knew that Renee's due date was coming up and how hard she took her miscarriage. I was so caught up in my shit that I couldn't be there for my best friend.

"Are you okay? Do you need anything?"

She softly smiled. "No, I'm good. It hit me hard the actual day, but now I'm doing better."

"I seriously feel like shit, Renee. I have been so caught up in my head these past few days that the date didn't even click with me. I'm sorry."

She nodded. "It's fine, Naudi. I swear."

Even though I could see she meant it, it didn't make me feel any better.

"Come on, I just cooked," she said, turning and heading to the back of her house. Since I didn't eat this morning, that was music to my ears.

"Matt stopped by," Renee said when we sat down on the couch with our food.

I rolled my eyes. "For what?"

"He wanted to be here for me since it was my due date."

"I hope you told him to go to hell."

"You know I did. I told his ass don't come back to my house. I don't know why he just can't take the hint."

My phone vibrated on my lap. I grabbed it and looked at the screen.

Smacking my lips, I locked it and placed the phone back on my lap. "Who is that?" Renee raised her eyebrow.

I sighed. "Tariq and Danny."

"You and Tariq into it?"

"Girl, fuck him." I licked my lips then brought the fork to my mouth to take a bite of the food.

Oddly, this was the first time Tariq had reached out to me since I left his house. I wasn't shocked though; Tariq wasn't the type to beg anyone. Danny, however, had been hitting me up once in a while, and sometimes I would entertain a conversation with him, but right now, I wasn't in the mood.

"What happened?"

"It doesn't matter. Right now is about you," I waved her question off.

"Naudia, I'm fine. What happened?"

Seeing she wasn't going to let up, I quickly ran down what happened with Tariq and me. "So now what? You're just giving up on yall?"

I looked at her like she was crazy. "What else am I supposed to do, Renee? He lied to me and it's obvious he still wants Chyna. I'm not competing with her." I rolled my eyes at her question.

"Okay, that's his girlfriend though, Naudia. You can't expect him to easily let go of their relationship even if the two of you have a connection."

"I'm not seeing you're point." I gave her a blank stare.

"You always deal with guys that have girlfriends without concern for the girlfriends. You finally catch feelings for one of them and get upset that he couldn't easily let go of the relationship he was in. You may not like Chyna, but Tariq wasn't wrong for sleeping with her."

I snickered and shook my head. "You know what," I stood up and set my plate next to me on the table, "I'm going to leave," I told her.

She frowned. "I know your ass isn't mad."

"Tariq played me, and yet you're defending Chyna. What do you think?" I gave her another blank stare.

"That was his girlfriend. Tariq wasn't your nigga, Naudi!"

"So what! We agreed that we were going to be together. Just forget it, I won't make a mistake like that again. I'll talk to you later." I picked up my purse off of the ground.

Renee called out to me, but I ignored her. If she felt so bad for Chyna, then she could go be friends with that bitch.

———

"SHIT NICK!" I yelled, pushing his head down. I threw my head back as my toes curled.

After leaving Renee's house, I received a text from Nick. I hadn't talked to him in a while since I was trying to stay away from anyone that wasn't Tariq, but that was out the window.

Nick's tongue flicked over my clit then he pulled it into his mouth. His fingers plunged in and out of me quickly.

"Ahhhh," I yelled, tightening my pussy around his fingers.

Nick pulled my clit into his mouth one last time before I was releasing in his mouth. My body shook and I grabbed his sheets, panting wildly.

"Damn," I mumbled, looking down at Nick kissing up my body. When he got to my breasts, he pulled on one nipple while massaging the other. When he bit down, I jumped.

"I missed you," he said.

I slid my tongue into his mouth and grabbed his face. "I want to feel you," I mumbled.

Nick nodded and pulled up. He reached over and grabbed the condom that was waiting for him. Quickly ripping it open, he placed it on his dick then placed it at my entrance.

Covering my mouth with his, he kissed me again then pushed

himself in me. I closed my eyes as I tried not to tense up.

Sex with Nick was always good, but something felt different this time. He moved in and out of me while kissing on my neck. I closed my eyes trying to push the nagging feeling out of my mind.

My legs went around his back. I started matching his strokes. Nick licked his thumb then started rubbing on my clit.

"Nick!" I yelled, feeling myself about to cum again. He began rubbing it faster, causing me to release again.

Nick unwrapped my legs from around him then pulled out of me.

"Get on all fours," he said.

He bit down on his bottom lip and stared at me lustfully.

I looked over his naked body until my eyes fell on his dick. He made it jump and I quickly turned over. Nick grabbed my hips and pushed back into me.

Instantly I started throwing my ass back at him. I lowered my head and gripped the sheets once Nick started matching my thrusts.

"Damn, baby!" he moaned, slapping my ass cheeks. I felt him spread them so that he could push deeper inside me.

Nick slowed his strokes up and pushed deeper into me.

He grabbed my hair and yanked my head back. "This pussy good as hell," he mumbled.

Nick and I kept going at it until we both came one last time. Nick pulled out of me and turned me over. He laid on me and kissed me.

His big hands massaged my breasts.

For some reason, this sex session with Nick felt different. I wasn't sure why or what it was.

"How come you keep avoiding me, Naudia?" Nick started kissing on my neck.

"I'm not." I fidgeted under him.

"Yeah, you do. What some nigga had your attention?" He pulled away and stared down at me.

My mind shifted to Tariq. Even with me sleeping with Nick didn't take away from the hurt he caused.

"Nick, you're tripping." I pushed him off me and sat up.

I could feel him staring at the side of my face.

"You don't get tired of this?" he asked.

"What?"

"Fucking around." He cuffed my neck.

I closed my eyes and my body shuttered.

"I don't know what you mean, Nick," I sighed softly.

Nick stopped kissing me and my eyes immediately opened. He stared at me like he was conflicted with something. "What's wrong?" I scrunched my face up.

"Why don't we stop all this in-between shit and make things work with us?"

"With us?" I repeated.

"Yeah, this open relationship or whatever we called ourselves having was cool at first, but I don't want that shit anymore."

"Nick," I groaned and stood up.

"That's not something you want?"

I didn't look at him. Instead, I started getting dressed. "No, Nick. You know I don't want a relationship." Once again, my mind went to Tariq, but I shook those thoughts away.

Nick got up and wrapped his arms around me. "Alright, I hear you. Chill out. It was just a thought. No need for you to leave." Nick pulled my clothes from my hands, tossing them to the side.

Gently pushing me on his bed, he hovered over me. "I'm not done with you," he said while slowly kissing down my body.

I knew I should probably leave, but Nick's lips on my body had me paralyzed. I knew he could normally go for a few rounds, so I wasn't shocked. Even though I didn't want to be with him in that way, I wouldn't turn down having sex with him.

CHAPTER 6

TARIQ

"ALRIGHT, SO WE HAVE A PROBLEM," I TOLD BRADY AND LUCAS.

They both looked up at me. "Man, I already know you're about to say some bullshit." Lucas shook his head.

I sighed and nodded. "Not only are we being looked at for the gambling shit but drugs as well."

Lucas turned his face up. "Drugs? The fuck for?"

"I don't know. My cousin is finding out what he can from the files through the database, but it's been hard because the DEA is targeting us."

"Shit," Brady mumbled.

Lucas and I turned to face him. "What's up?" I asked him.

Brady gripped the back of his neck. "I didn't think it was a big deal because we been bringing in more money and it wasn't hurting anyone, but I guess that shit wasn't true." Brady shook his head.

"Nigga, what you do?" Lucas asked.

"I been selling pills out of here. That's where some of the extra income came from."

"Nigga what the fuck!" I yelled jumping up.

"I thought we agreed we wasn't doing that shit!" Lucas snapped.

"No one knew about it. I stayed under the radar, plus it brought in a lot of money. I didn't think it was a big deal." Brady shrugged.

"Well, obviously, it was because now we're being looked at even harder! That's why they been pushing this undercover shit!" I yelled.

Fuck man. The last thing we needed was this kind of attention. The regular detectives were one thing, but the DEA was a whole 'nother ball game.

"I don't see how the nigga even found out. I kept the shit under wraps. I made sure no one ran their mouths, and I personally knew who was getting the pills."

"That shit doesn't matter now, does it? We're fucking being investigated for drugs now. That shit is bigger than illegal gambling!" Spit flew out of Lucas's mouth he was so pissed.

Lucas started pacing back and forth. "How much are you selling out of here?" I asked Brady.

"At first, it was about thirty grand a week, but since we moved locations and have more people coming in, it's tripled. So now it's close to a hundred grand." I choked, and Lucas stopped pacing and glared at him.

"Nigga, you really were on some sneaky shit! A hundred fucking grand!"

"I wasn't on no sneaky shit! All the money I made I put in with the money in the safe! Yall think our numbers increased from this casino alone!" Brady mugged Lucas. You could tell he was offended by his words.

"And you didn't think to say shit! Look at where the fuck we are now!"

"Nigga, at the end of the day, I'm grown as fuck. Can't nobody tell me not to do shit. If I was a grimy nigga, I would have kept the money for myself, but I made sure yall niggas ate too!"

Brady walked out of the room. I looked at Lucas and he looked pissed off. "This nigga tripping." I shook my head.

Even though I was happy about the extra income coming in, I wasn't trying to go to jail for the shit.

"I knew that nigga was on some bullshit," Lucas finally said.

Brady soon appeared again and threw a bag at Lucas. "What the fuck is this?" Lucas mugged him.

"Look inside." Brady nodded.

Lucas looked at me. "Shit, open it," I shrugged.

Lucas opened the bag. "What's this?"

"The money we made the past two weeks. I separated it into threes already. I planned on telling yall about the pills. I wanted to figure out what yall wanted to do with everything going on."

Lucas looked up from the bag. I could see the wheels in his head spinning.

"No one was on no shady shit. Besides me not telling yall, I made sure the money was divided evenly.

Lucas handed me the bag and I looked inside. "So what are we going to do now?" Lucas finally asked.

I couldn't lie and say that I was trying to give up the extra money we had coming in, but I wasn't sure if it was worth the risk.

"Let's ask Brady since he thought this shit out." Brady mugged me. I was annoyed as hell.

"I'm not trying to stop the pills. We need to find out the undercover and handle him," Brady said.

"Shit, me neither," I looked at Lucas.

"Is it worth the risk?"

"Hell, the nigga been doing it this long. Doesn't really matter at this point."

I looked between Brady and Lucas. I could see they were both on the same page.

"Fuck it. If yall want to keep this shit going, then I'm down." I shrugged.

Both of them nodded. "Just chill out for a few weeks and let the attention die down," I said.

I would hit my cousin up and give him the heads up so he can try to help us.

We went over numbers and how we were going to handle this pill shit. I couldn't lie and say I wasn't lowkey side-eyeing Brady. I felt like he was on some funny shit but to see that he was dividing the money put some of those thoughts to rest.

"Aye, where that nigga Trevor been?" Brady asked as we started setting up for the night.

I noticed Lucas's face grow tight. "That nigga better be headed back to Chicago if he knows what's good for him."

"The fuck happened with yall?"

Lucas clenched his jaw. "Found out some shit with him and Trinity."

I furrowed my eyebrows together. "What shit?"

Lucas gave me a knowing look. "Hell nah. Not Trinity."

"Yeah, man, heard that shit with my own two ears." He ran his tongue over his top teeth.

"And you ain't put a bullet in that nigga?" Brady asked.

"Shit, I wanted to. Wanted to put one in both they heads. I couldn't do that to Trinity or my daughter though. I beat his ass and told him if I saw him again, I was shooting."

I shook my head. "Damn, that nigga grimy as hell for that shit."

"It's cool. I'll get at him again eventually. I should have known that nigga was disloyal. Any nigga that steals can't be trusted."

Lucas turned around and started setting back up the station he was working on. Him mentioning disloyalty made me think of mine and Naudia's situation. She wasn't fucking with me right now, but that didn't mean I didn't want to still try and make us work. I hadn't talked to Chyna since she left my house either.

I needed a break from both women at the moment. "Aye Lucas, I need to holla at you," I told him, causing him to look over at me frowning.

"Man, if you about to tell me some more bullshit, then save it."

I shook my head. "Nah, nothing like that."

————

AFTER LEAVING from meeting with the guys, I stopped by Chyna's house. She had texted me asking if we could talk and I figured I put it off for too long.

"Oh, look, it's my loving boyfriend," Chyna's voice dripped with sarcasm.

"If you wanted me to come here to be on some bullshit, then I can leave," I told her, stepping past her in the house.

When I turned to face her, she had her arms crossed over her chest. A smug look was on her face. I could tell she had a lot on her mind.

"What is it, Chyna?"

Her eyes narrowed. "I want you to tell me the truth."

Crossing my arms, my face went blank. "About what?"

"That little fast ass Naudia. Is there something going on with you two?"

"Something like what? Damn, why you always bringing her up?" I was tired of this always being a constant argument between the two of us. Even though I had slipped up twice with Naudia, I made sure Chyna never felt like I was pushing her to the side, well at least I thought I did.

"Are you fucking her?" Chyna threw her hands up then placed them on her hips.

"Why would you ask me some shit like that?"

"Because every time she comes around yall two act like it. You always take her side whenever we get into it. Then the last time I was at your house you kicked me out right in the middle of us having sex!"

"Yall two started fighting! What the hell else was I supposed to do?"

"Make her leave. I'm your girlfriend. I don't get why her feelings are always put over mine."

I stared at Chyna and saw she was really upset. I could tell she was fighting back tears. Hurting her wasn't something I wanted to do, and I knew it wasn't fair for me to keep stringing her along, knowing I wanted someone else either. Even though I cared about Chyna, my feelings for Naudia were growing every day too. It was getting harder to fight them, and in the end, both girls were getting hurt, which I didn't want.

I was too old to be juggling two different girls. Most niggas would like that shit, but I didn't. That was something I did when I was younger. Now it was time for me to man up.

"Look, Chyna," I started trying to figure out the right words.

The tears she had been battling finally won and fell down her face like she knew what I was about to say.

"Maybe we need to chill for a little bit," I finally said.

Her mouth slightly parted. "Chill? Why?"

I tugged on my beard and released a deep breath. "I don't want to keep stringing you on. I'm not going to lie to you either. I have feelings for Naudia and-"

"You have feelings for her? How the fuck do you have feelings for someone you never been with, Tariq? What about us!"

"Stop yelling and let me finish!" Her mouth snapped closed, but she had a disdained look on her face.

"Now, like I was saying. I don't know when or how they started, but I started having feelings for Naudia. At first, I was fighting them because I didn't want to ruin what we had. I also didn't want to hurt you."

"So why are you now?" she cried.

"I'm not trying to do it. Naudia just, I don't know, man." I ran my hand down my face.

I honestly wasn't sure what it was that was pulling me to Naudia. Maybe the fact that I knew she was better than how she was acting or that I knew the real her.

"Tariq, I don't want to break up." I looked Chyna in the eyes. I didn't like that she was crying; that wasn't what I came here to do.

"It's not fair for me to be with you knowing I have feelings for another girl."

"Fuck her, Tariq! Her hoe ass done been with half the niggas in the area! Why would you want to be with someone like her?"

I clenched my jaw. "I'm not going to explain myself to you. I said what I had to say."

"So what you're going to go be with her?"

I shook my head. "Nah, I'm not dealing with either of you right now."

I walked up to Chyna and pulled her into me. "I'm not doing this to hurt you, Chyna. I just need to figure shit out."

She slowly nodded her head and wrapped her arms around me.

"I love you, Tariq, but I can't promise I'll be waiting around for you to choose." I licked my lips and thought over her words.

Of course, I didn't want Chyna with anyone else, but it would be selfish for me to expect her to wait for a nigga.

"Do what you got to do." I kissed her forehead and let her go.

Stepping around her, I walked towards the front door. "Just

remember the type of girl you're leaving me for," she said behind me.

I grabbed her door and pulled it open, not bothering to respond. Chyna could continue to try and paint Naudia a certain way, but I knew it was more to her than that.

CHAPTER 7

BRADY

"So what are you saying?" Tech asked me, staring at me confused.

"I need to cut back on the number of pills I'm getting from you," I told him.

His eyebrows bunched together. "I don't get it. I thought that we were making good money together?" Tech looked away from the computer in front of him, giving me his full attention.

I stared at him with a blank expression. I wasn't about to put out the issues we were having. I didn't want Tech to pull out this deal fully, but until Tariq got more information from his cousin, we needed to stay under the radar as much as possible. Selling a large quantity of pills like I was before would cause the DEA to lock in on us even more. I wasn't trying to be the reason why everything we worked for blew up in our face.

"Shits just been hectic and it's just better this way for now."

Tech looked like he wanted to go against what I was saying, but if he knew what was good for him, he'd accept what I just said. It wasn't like I was cutting all ties with him I was just cutting back.

"Look, regardless of what the reason is, it's happening. We'll still be doing business together, just not as much as before. I don't know how long it's going to last, but you better be happy I'm still doing any business at all." I pushed my seat back and stood up.

"I'll hit you up once I get rid of all this."

Tech kept a mug on his face but nodded.

After this pick-up, the money might slow down, but hopefully, it would get the DEA off our back.

———

I was sitting outside the warehouse when my phone went off. I looked down and was shocked to see it was my mom calling. It had been a few weeks since I'd talked to her.

"What's up, ma?" I asked when I heard sniffling on the other end. "Mama? What's wrong?" I could feel my anger flaring up.

"Son?" she struggled out.

"I'm here. You okay?"

"Your father is meeting with the parole board next week."

I licked my lips and stared at the scenery in front of me. "There's no reason to cry over that though, mama."

"What if they let him out?" she cried.

"That nigga almost took your life. If they let him go, then they're a bunch of fools. They've denied him every time before now, and this time shouldn't be any different. It's going to be okay." I tried to calm her down.

Her breathing slowed down on the phone. I could hear her cries getting softer too. "I just don't know what I'll do if they let him out."

"They won't. You're safe and away from him. Don't worry."

"Okay, I'm sorry for bothering you."

That made me smile. "Come on, mama, you know you're no bother. I'ma come out there to see you this weekend, alright?" I told her.

"Don't say it and then don't do it, Brady," I chuckled.

"Now you know I wouldn't lie to you. I'll be there."

"Okay, well I guess I'll be seeing you this weekend."

We spoke a little longer before hanging up the phone.

I sighed and laid my head back on my seat. Just the mention of my dad made me want to break into the prison and put one between his eyes. That nigga was selfish and used to treat me and my mom like a punching bag for most of my life.

Every time it was time for his parole hearing my mom would start freaking out. I always had to remind her she didn't have anything to worry about. She always wrote the parole board begging them to keep him locked up. It's been years since he's been out of our lives, yet my mom was still terrified of him. That shit pissed me off. There was no reason why my mom should fear anyone. If I had the opportunity to end his life, I would, no questions.

I felt myself getting into one of my moods and knew I needed to calm down. Sometimes my anger got the best of me and now wasn't the time for that.

I got out of the car and walked to the back of my car to grab the pills.

Once I was in the warehouse I went straight back to the office.

"Glad yall could meet me," I told Tariq and Lucas.

They looked up at me. "Nigga this better be important?" Lucas bucked.

I mugged him. "Here's the order of pills I just got from Tech." I walked to the desk in the room and sat the bag down, then opened it.

Both Lucas and Tariq surrounded me to look. "I thought we were cutting back," Tariq said.

"This is the last big order. I figured since the word is out about them, it's time for me to fill yall in how I run things."

They both looked at each other and nodded.

I spent the next ten minutes explaining my pill operation.

"Damn, I can't lie and say that shit ain't smooth," Tariq chuckled and looked at the pills again.

"Yeah, now I see how yo ass kept under the radar even from us," Lucas joined in.

"Exactly, that's why I'm surprised we're being investigated."

"Fuck that shit though. Whoever the nigga is gone get handled along with the nigga talking." We all nodded.

Lucas pulled his phone out and I could see his jaw clench. He cleared the call and slipped the phone back in his pocket.

"You good?"

"Yeah, that was just Trinity."

"You still not fucking with her?" I asked.

"Nah," he kept it short.

I looked at Tariq and he shrugged.

"Anyway. Let's get these pills sorted so we can start setting up for tonight," Lucas said, sitting at the desk.

The three of us started getting the pills ready so it would be easier to sell them then we headed out to the floor.

The bullshit with my dad was still heavy on my mind, but I tried to push it to the back. I knew they weren't going to let that nigga out, so I wasn't worried.

CHAPTER 8

RENEE

"YOU STILL UPSET?" I WALKED UP TO THE TABLE WHERE NAUDIA was sitting in the middle of the quad.

She looked up from the paper she was reading over. "Who said I was upset?"

Her eyes went back to the paper.

I took a seat next to her. "Come on, I know you, Naudia. You got mad at what I said to you that day."

She looked at me and rolled her eyes. "I didn't get mad because of what you said. I got mad because what you said was true." She licked her lips then looked off to the side. "Chyna is Tariq's girlfriend and I shouldn't be mad about what happened." She shrugged, then looked back at me.

"True, but I should have been more considerate. I know you really like Tariq." she waved me off.

"Girl, it wasn't that deep."

I laughed. "Yeah, whatever. Have you talked to him?"

"For what? He can stay where he's at with his girlfriend."

"Okay, keep telling yourself that."

Things grew quiet between us. "Have you put any thought into your birthday?" I asked her.

Naudia smiled widely. "I just want to go out and party for real. Maybe rent a section out and have everyone come."

I nodded. "What about your brother and Trinity? She told me how things went south for them."

I spoke to Trinity a few days ago and she sounded upset. When she told me what was wrong, I was blown away. The way she was with Lucas, I would have never guessed she would do something like that.

"Hell, Lucas and her will just have to put their differences to the side. He can't even be mad. He tried to play her out at that party. He's just in his feelings."

I got what Naudia was saying, but I didn't think it was that easy. "Yeah, but you know how your brother is."

"He'll be good," she waved me off.

Her eyes traveled around the quad again. "This is my lucky day!" Naudia started to gather all her stuff up and stuff it in her book bag.

"Where are you going?" I asked, getting up behind her.

"To slap this bitch!" she said.

I stared at her confused then looked around until my eyes fell on Kelsey.

"Come on, Naudia, not here," I tried to tell her.

She had got caught fighting a few times on campus and was already put on probation for that and her grades. If she got in trouble again, I was sure they'd kick her out of her program.

Naudia being Naudia, ignored me and walked up to Kelsey, grabbing her shoulder.

"Remember me bitch!" she yelled, dropping her book bag and throwing a punch.

Kelsey looked stunned at first, not expecting the hit, but she quickly shook it off. She went to hit Naudia, but Naudia threw another punch.

"Your friends should have told you I was looking for your

stupid ass. You like leaving people at parties, huh?" Naudia had her by her hair. She lifted her knee and sent it against Kelsey's face.

People had surrounded the two fighting. A lot of them were recording and cheering the fight on.

"Naudi, that's enough. Come on," I yelled, trying to get her to stop. I noticed security coming our way. Naudia didn't let up though.

I grabbed her arm and tried to pull her away, but it was too late security had already walked up on us.

"Fuck," I mumbled, watching them break the fight up.

Naudia was laughing at Kelsey, who was yelling and trying to break free.

The security guards carried both of the girls away while I picked up Naudia's bag and went to my car to wait.

———

"Lucas is going to fuck me up," Naudia groaned and grabbed her head.

We had stopped by a small local sandwich shop up the street.

"Hell yeah, he's going to be pissed." Naudia lifted her face to look at me frowning.

"That's not what I need right now."

"Hell, you knew if you fought one more time, they were going to kick you out of school. You should have caught that hoe another time."

"I never even wanted to go to college for real," she mumbled, picking her sandwich up.

"What are you going to tell him then?" she shrugged.

"Nothing. At least not right now. It's only a few more weeks left in the semester for real, so I'll figure it out before the next semester starts."

"Aye, you did beat her ass though, friend." Me and Naudia laughed.

"I told you them hoes had to see me on site. What if something bad would have happened to me that night?"

"True. Something good came out of it though."

She looked at me confused. "What?"

"You got to stay the night at your man's house."

She smacked her lips. "Yeah, but his girlfriend was there."

I smirked. "You gone keep on fronting, huh?"

"Bye Renee. Let's talk about you and Brady. You two seem to be getting really cozy."

I bit down on my bottom lip. "What can I say? Brady isn't the playboy I thought he was. Or at least not anymore."

"I'm sure Brady is passed that. You two are good together."

I smiled at her words. Since the day I was down about my due date, Brady made sure to stop by or call me to see how I was doing. I also had started putting more effort in on my end. I realized I used to push Brady away or distance myself from him because I was scared of being hurt, but Brady never showed me that he would do me wrong. In fact, he was so into me that whenever I hurt, he took that pain on too.

I never had that with Matt. With Brady, I felt a strong connection even when we first started to have sex. No matter what he was doing, he would drop everything to check on me too.

Still, a small part of me was waiting for the other shoe to drop and something bad to happen. I hoped it wouldn't happen, but I couldn't be too sure.

CHAPTER 9

LUCAS

"See something you like?" Brandy looked over her shoulder at me.

I stared at her bending over in front of the bar to pick something up off the floor. As usual, she was dressed in some small spandex shorts. Her ass cheeks were threatening to fall out of them.

Brandy had a lot of sex appeal and she wasn't scared to show it off either. It was one reason she made a good employee. The niggas ate her up.

It had been a while since I slid in something. Since Trinity left me, I wasn't fucking with her anymore, which had me backed up.

"Shit, I got some tension I need to relieve. You gone help me do that?" Brandy stood straight up, turned around to face me, and looked at my center.

"I'm tired of just sucking your dick," she frowned.

I smirked. "Good thing I want more than just my dick sucked." I nodded in the direction of the office, and just like I thought, Brandy followed behind me.

After we entered the office, I went behind the desk and opened one of the drawers to grab a condom.

"What changed?" Brandy asked, stripping out her clothes. I took her naked body in. She was stacked in clothes, but out of them, Brandy was killing shit.

My mind went to Trinity, and I knew if she knew I was doing this, she would be hurt. But then visions of her and Trevor popped in my head, pushing all those thoughts out.

"Don't ask me any questions. Bend over the desk," I told her while undoing my pants.

Once I secured the condom on my dick and walked to the other side of the desk. Brandy was gripping the edge of the desk. Her fat ass was facing me.

I slapped it with my hands then reached around her to play with her pussy. "She's ready for you. I've been wanting this for a while," Brandy moaned.

I ignored her and moved my hand. Grabbing my dick, I placed it at her entrance. Brandy threw her hips backwards as I spread her ass cheeks and pushed inside her.

"Shit," she moaned.

Holding her hips, I started moving in and out of her. Brandy's pussy was decent, nothing to brag about. The good thing was she was wet and threw her ass back like a pro.

I grabbed the back of her neck and squeezed it while drilling into her from behind. Brandy's moans became louder, but I drowned them out. She kept throwing her ass back and soon began cumming.

"Lucas!" she yelled, going faster.

Her pussy gripped my dick tighter and it became wetter. Moving my hands from her neck, I grabbed her hips and circled my hips into her.

As soon as I knew she was done cumming, I snatched out of her.

"Finish me off." I nodded down at my dick, taking the condom off.

Brandy licked her lips and dropped down, taking me in her mouth. I closed my eyes and grabbed her head so I could guide her motions. I pushed my dick deeper in her mouth and she took it like a champ.

"Fuck! I groaned, shooting my seeds down her throat.

Brandy continued sucking me until I didn't have anything left. I quickly snatched my dick out of her mouth and stepped back.

"You can go." I walked over to where my pants and boxers were to put them on.

"Damn, it's like that," she frowned.

"How else was it supposed to be?" I gave her a blank look.

She rolled her eyes. "At least I know your dick is good, just like I thought," she smiled and started getting dressed.

I ignored what she said. "Hopefully, this won't be the only time."

"Go handle the bar, Brandy." She smacked her lips then headed out the office. I walked over to the bathroom that was in the office to wash my hands.

Fucking Brandy helped me release some sexual frustration, but I was still irritated. I walked back to the desk and grabbed my phone. My screensaver was a picture of Trinity and Lucia sleep in the bed. I had come home one night to see them laying in our bed, and I snapped the off-guard picture.

Just staring at Trinity sleeping on my screen and seeing how peaceful and innocent she looked pissed me off. Knowing that face was full of lies angered me.

I locked my screen and tossed my phone back on the desk. Trinity had me off my game for the past month. Now it was time to get back to it.

———

"How we looking tonight?" I asked Tariq.

He had already been to the safe to put some money away and I'm sure he might have to make a second trip.

"Shit, good as hell. Tonight is for sure a money-making night." I smiled and rubbed my hands together. Knowing we were under the watchful eyes of the DEA had all three of us on edge, but it wasn't slowing down our money. We had sold all the pills Brady got from his last order and now were offering smaller amounts. We had kept him in charge of all that since he knew what was going on with it already.

I turned and headed back on the floor.

Tonight was pretty packed. We were having a ladies' night, so it was a lot of females in the building along with the usual crowd of niggas.

I looked around the place and my eyes fell on a beauty at the bar. She had just turned to the bar to place an order and her backside was poking out like crazy. Licking my lips, I turned and made my way over.

"I know yo pretty ass ain't in here gambling." The girl turned to face me frowning before her face lit up.

"Hey, Lucas!" She smiled and hugged me.

I chuckled and hugged her waist. "What's up, girl." She let me go. I took her in and noticed how she'd really grown up since I last saw her.

I used to mess around with Alisha back in the day.

"How have you been? You here gambling?"

I looked at her offended. "Girl, what? This is my place." Her eyes widened.

"Is it really?"

I nodded. "Me, Brady, and Tariq."

"Shut up. You guys done really came up, huh." I smirked and nodded again.

"What you doing here? Last I check yo nigga had you under lock and key."

She rolled her eyes and smacked her lips. "I left his broke ass."

"Still only chasing a bag, huh?" I laughed.

"No, but I mean, don't no woman want a broke nigga that she has to take care of." I couldn't fault her there. "What about you? You're still with Trinity, right?"

My face went blank and I ran my tongue over my top teeth. "Nah, we broke up."

"For now, I remember how yall used to be."

"Nah, for good." I looked her in the eyes.

"Did you need something?" Brandy came over asking with tons of attitude laced in her voice. She looked between me and Alisha, frowning.

"Take that fucking attitude out yo voice," I warned her.

Alisha looked at her and giggled. "I don't want anything from you."

"Go ahead, Brandy." I waved her off and waved another bartender over.

"Look, I got to get back to the floor. Let me get yo number and Ima hit you up."

Alisha smiled bashfully and nodded. I went in my pocket and she read off her number. "Bet, I locked you in and sent you mine. I'll hit you up."

I looked her over one last time before shaking my head and walking away.

Alisha has always been fine as hell. If I didn't get with Trinity, I would have been with her. She was light-skinned with long brown hair, thick pink lips, and a small mole right above her lip on the right side. She was stacked like fuck too. Her body reminded me of Buffy the Body. I didn't know if that shit was real, but it looked good.

The only flaw in her is she was a sack chaser. Back then I

wasn't making enough for her, but the dick was good, so she kept coming back.

It was funny that she walked in here tonight after I was done with Trinity. Maybe this was fate.

CHAPTER 10

TRINITY

"You gone make your boo fuck you up wearing that," I told Naudia looking at the dress she had in her hand.

"And your brother." Naudia and I rolled our eyes at that one.

"Girl, both of them better leave me alone. This is super cute."

"It's a table cloth," I joked.

Naudia smiled brightly. "A cute table cloth."

We were all shopping for her birthday. Even though I didn't want to be around Lucas, I wasn't going to miss out on whatever Naudia had planned. She informed me that she had rented out a section at this hookah bar, which was cool. The place was known to be pretty lit on the weekend after hours.

"Hell, it's your birthday. Do what you want." I shrugged, looking over the other dress options.

I knew I had to be on my Ps and Qs being around Lucas. He was still mad about finding out about me and Trevor, but I wasn't letting it get me down anymore. We didn't even speak anymore. He would walk Lucia to the door and turn to leave soon as I opened it or wait for me to open the door and drive off. It stung at first that he could so quickly write me off, but I had to learn to deal with it.

"I just want to enjoy my birthday by dancing and drinking then fall asleep after getting some good dick." Naudia started twerking where she was.

Both me and Renee laughed. "Yeah, you gone get cursed out by the end of the night," I said.

She waved me off. "All I know is I'm expecting you to turn up with me." Naudia grabbed my arm.

"What about me?" Renee frowned.

"Bitch I'm pretty sure Brady is going to come with my brother. Meaning your ass is going to be boo'd up."

"Okay, and I bet Tariq will be there too."

"What does that have to do with me? I haven't even talked to that man."

I side-eyed Naudia and removed my arm from hers. "Girl bye! As soon as Tariq get in yo ass you gone be singing a different tune."

Naudia smacked her lips.

"Anyway, I have a hair appointment in the morning, so it'll be freshly done. Then I need to get my nails done. Since I found my outfit, I'll be able to coordinate." She pulled the dress away from her and looked it over again.

I shook my head. I knew soon as the guys saw her in this they were going to go off, but Naudia didn't care about that. I actually think she enjoyed pissing them off at this point.

We spent the rest of the time going to different stores. I had to get back home for when Lucas brought Lucia home. Every time he dropped her off, I was nervous. He always looked at me like he hated me. Hopefully, today he stayed in the car and waited for me to open the door.

———

I CLOSED my eyes and took a deep breath before smiling and opening the door.

"Hey!" I said.

Lucas looked at me with a blank face. "Hi mommy!" Lucia ran in, hugging my waist, then ran back to her room.

I hated that she was getting so comfortable with our current arrangement.

Just when I was about to close the door, Lucas held his hand up, causing me to grow confused. "Did you need something?" I asked him.

"Let me use your bathroom." He didn't wait for me to answer.

He pushed the door open and made his way into my house.

"You didn't have to be rude," I mumbled, closing the door.

I walked into the living room and took a seat. For some reason, I was nervous about having Lucas in my house. I played on my phone for a while until I heard him clear his throat.

"Must be texting a nigga." He mugged me.

I looked up at him frowning. "What?"

"You still be talking to Trevor?" I swallowed hard.

"No, Lucas." I rolled my eyes and sat my phone down.

While he was standing there, I looked him over. I wish his ass would have looked stressed or something, but he didn't. He looked good and healthy.

"Lucia told me you grounded her." He took his phone out and smirked at whoever texted him. Jealously shot through me because I had a feeling it was a girl.

"Yeah, I did." I nodded.

He replied to the message then looked at me. "Why?"

I cocked my head back. "I didn't think I needed permission to ground my daughter."

"Lucia isn't a bad kid, so why the hell would you have to ground her?"

He looked at his phone and laughed before tapping the screen. "Are you going to take your attention off your phone and listen or not?" I snapped.

Lucas finished his text then looked at me smirking. "Why you ground her?" He slid his phone into his pocket.

"Because she got in trouble in school for the third time. She won't stop talking back, so I grounded her."

Lucas frowned. "You didn't think I needed to know that shit?"

"It's not like you paid attention to what was going on any other time. I handled it and she's been doing better."

I could tell Lucas was annoyed, but I didn't care. He was always too busy for everything, so I didn't see the need to tell him.

"When it comes to my damn child, I need to know Trinity! Don't start being on that dumb shit because you won't like how it plays out!" his voice got louder.

"Don't talk to me like I'm your damn kid!" I jumped up.

"Then stop being childish. If my daughter is getting in trouble in school, I need to know that. Don't start being a bitter baby mama."

"Bitter? Nigga I'm far from bitter."

"You heard what I said. Anything else happens with her, I expect to know." I didn't say anything. Lucas had his nerve coming in here talking to me like he was crazy.

"Whatever, Lucas, you can let yourself out." I rolled my eyes and sat down.

He stared down at me for a minute before taking his phone out and ignoring a call. "I really can't believe you had me fooled." He turned his lip up.

"I didn't have anyone fooled! You won't even let me explain."

"Ain't shit to explain. You fucked my homie. Case closed." I felt low when he spoke those words. They were true, but it wasn't like he thought.

"Lucas, me fucking Trevor was a mistake. It just happened," I started.

"I don't even want to hear this shit." He turned and walked towards the door. I jumped up and followed him.

"How many times did you fuck up and I took you back! How many times did I listen to you beg and plead that you wouldn't hurt me again? Now you can't even hear me out!"

"I never fucked your friend!" He stopped, turned around and yelled, causing me to jump.

"I'm sorry," I said lowly.

There was nothing else I could say. I know what I did was wrong, and I felt bad, but it was the past, and I just wanted Lucas to move past it.

"You had to get a test on my damn daughter, Tri. I can't forget that." I dropped my head and ran my hand through my hair.

"Mommy, I'm hungry," Lucia ran into the room and yelled.

I quickly wiped my eyes and looked up at her. "Okay, I'll make you something."

I looked at Lucas one last time, and he still had a frown on his face. "Daddy are you staying?" Lucia asked, running up to us.

"Nah, baby, I got stuff to do, but I'll see you in a few days." He bent down and kissed her cheek.

He stood up and didn't give me a second look as he walked out the door.

———

"WHEN THE HELL yo ass started getting hips!" I yelled at Naudia walking into the section she had rented out. Her birthday was tomorrow, but she was celebrating it tonight since it was a weekend.

"Girl, don't play!" She laughed and downed her drink.

Naudia looked good.

The dress she had on was more so a crop top and high-waisted skirt. It was nude, and she was wearing a black thong with a black laced bra. The top of the dress circled her neck and was sleeveless. It was really cute but very provocative.

"Bitch you look good as hell!" Renee yelled, hugging Naudia.

Naudia had also got her hair to straighten and was wearing it half up in a high ponytail and the rest cascaded down her back. Renee was also wearing a two-piece dress set, but hers wasn't see-through. It was red with the top cut low, and the bottom had a high slit. I settled on a cute crop top and high-waisted jeans with some wedges.

Naudia poured another drink and looked around. "I done seen a few cuties in here tonight. I'm finding my man tonight," she laughed and threw her drink back. I shook my head.

"Naudi, please don't show your ass tonight and don't overdo the drinking."

"It's my birthday! I'm fucking it up all night!"

She put the cup down and got on the couch and started twerking. Renee and I laughed and cheered her on. As long as she was in the section around us, then it was cool.

We all laughed and continued to drink as the hookah bar started to fill. The dance floor had just opened was started to get packed, and we had just ordered a hookah.

Naudia was still dancing when a voice made her freeze. "Who the fuck told you to wear some shit like that out the house!" She sat straight up and jumped off the couch as Tariq stormed to her.

I shook my head again. I knew this wasn't going to be good.

I looked behind Tariq and saw Brady come in and go right to Renee. Even though I shouldn't have, I looked for Lucas.

I was starting to think he hadn't arrived yet, but my eyes finally fell on him. My eyes bucked and my heart sunk seeing him walking up to the section with a girl. His arm was securely around her waist as if he was showing she was his.

I wasn't sure how to take this. I knew I would see Lucas tonight, but I didn't expect to see him with another girl on his arm.

CHAPTER 11

NAUDIA

Tariq and I stood in a standoff. He looked me over again and his frown deepened.

"Answer my damn question, Naudia. Why the fuck are you dressed like that?"

I rolled my eyes. "Tariq, leave me alone and go worry about your girlfriend." I tried to step around him.

"I swear you make a nigga want to fuck you up. You're basically fucking naked, Naudia!"

"Okay, so what!" I yelled back. "I'm covered where I need to be!"

Tariq's grip tightened. He yanked me into him and brought his mouth to my ear. "You show your ass one time tonight and I promise you I'm embarrassing you. You be in any nigga's face and I'm embarrassing you. Act like you got some fucking sense and I'm not playing."

His assertiveness turned me on. My knees buckled as his breath brushed against my ear.

"You can't tell me what to do," I said, trying to pull away.

He pulled me tighter. "Play with me if you want to. That shit is sexy though. I lowkey want to take you in the bathroom and rip it off you." My breathing sped up. Now he was playing. I had to remember I was mad at him

This was my first time seeing Tariq since I left his house, and instead of me holding on to my attitude, I was ready to fuck his ass.

"Whatever, Tariq. Let me go." He chuckled and kissed my cheek. "Happy birthday, beautiful." He finally let me go and I had to get myself together. I grew wet as hell as soon as he started talking. I licked my lips and he smirked, causing me to roll my eyes.

I walked away and went over to Trinity and realized she looked upset. "What's wrong?' I asked her, then followed her eyes.

"Oh, hell no!" I yelled.

I went to walk over to my brother, but she grabbed me. "Fuck him, sis."

"Hell no, I didn't make this a plus one."

I snatched away from her and stormed over to Lucas. "Who the hell is this, Lucas!" I yelled, mugging the girl he was holding around the waist.

"Sis, this is- yo what the fuck you got on!" He let the girl go.

"That's not important. Who the hell told you to bring some stray with you when you knew Trinity would be here!"

"Stray?" The girl cocked her head back.

"Did I stutter?" I asked, not backing down.

Lucas pushed the girl back and stood in front of her. The scowl on his face would normally affect me, but I could care less right now.

"First off, me and Trinity are over. I can be with whoever I want."

"Not at my damn gathering you can't! I don't know her!" I threw my hands up.

"Fuck all that. Why the fuck you come out the house in your damn underwear?" I looked down.

"I have on a dress."

"Where the fuck is the dress, Naudia? See you still doing this shit! You thought because it was your birthday that dressing like this was cool."

I smacked my lips. "I'm about to be twenty-three, Lucas! I'm old enough to dress how I want!"

"And what about the attention you get from dressing like that? How many times do I have to tell you that shit isn't cute?"

"How many times do I have to tell you I don't care!"

"Naudia, come on." Trinity walked over and grabbed my arm, pulling me away.

"Yo ass probably encouraged her to wear this shit," Lucas scolded, looking at Trinity.

"Fuck you, Lucas." Trinity pulled me away.

"I'm so sick of that nigga always thinking he's my daddy!" I went to the table and grabbed a bottle opening it.

"Happy birthday, sis. You not holding back, huh?" Brady asked, walking up and hugging me.

I giggled. "You know me!"

The servers brought the hookahs to the sections and we each took turns smoking from them; the girls, that is. The guys rolled up and smoked.

"Let me get a hit," I sat on the other side of Brady and asked.

He looked in Lucas's direction and I smacked my lips. "Don't do that." I snatched the blunt from him, causing him to laugh.

I took a few hits off the blunt before giving it back to him. "Want to go dance?" I looked at Renee and asked.

She nodded. I turned and went over to Trinity and pulled her up. "Come on. I'm not about to let you be in your feelings all night because of my dickhead brother."

Lucas and that girl had been on each other all night. She

hadn't left off his lap in the past hour, and they were making me gag for real.

"I'm not in my feelings," she argued.

"Shit, I can't tell. Come on."

The three of us headed for the entrance of the section, but Tariq stopped us. "Naudia, remember what I said." I looked at him.

"Daddy about to get her ass," Renee snickered.

"Ain't no one worried about him." I grabbed both their hands and kept walking.

The dance floor was full as hell compared to when we first got here, not to mention the music was on point. I was tipsy but not in a sloppy way. I was having a good time though.

The bottle girls delivered a bottle with sparklers to the table for my birthday, and the DJ had shouted me out, causing guys to send shots to the section. Most of them, Tariq made sure to decline, but I was able to sneak a few.

The three of us danced on the dance floor for a few songs. Renee kept turning guys down because of Brady, but Trinity surprisingly danced with a few. I was happy she was getting out of her feelings and enjoying herself.

"Come on, let's go to the bar," I told them.

I wanted the three of us to take a shot.

We walked over to the bar and I ordered a round of shots. "Damn, you just went MIA on a nigga, huh?"

I turned around and frowned seeing Danny behind me smiling. "Pretty much." I turned back around.

"To my birthday!" I yelled, raising the shot glass.

"Happy Birthday, bitch!" Renee and Trinity yelled. We all threw the shots back and I shook my head at the taste.

"Come on, let's go back to the section. I want to smoke the hookah some more," Renee suggested.

"Chill with me for a minute." Danny grabbed my arm as we went to walk away. I looked down at his hand on me and frowned.

"Naudia?" Trinity asked, staring at me curiously.

"Go ahead. I'll be there in a minute."

"You sure? We don't know him."

"Yeah, Naudi. We don't need the guys flipping out."

"Yall can see me from the section. Plus, I know him. It's all good." They nodded and turned to walk away.

"What you want to drink?" I turned to look at Danny. He still was cute as hell. Too bad he was wack in bed.

I ordered the drink I wanted then looked around the building.

"How old you turning?" he asked.

"Twenty-three."

"You looking good."

"I know," I smiled, then turned to face the crowd again.

Danny ran his hand down my arm making me jump. "What are you doing?"

He handed me my shot. "Why you start acting funny after we fucked?" I sipped the drink then looked at him.

"Just wasn't feeling it anymore," I shrugged.

"You weren't feeling it?" Danny looked confused.

I shrugged. "Nope." I downed the shot and set the glass back down.

"I want to dance though. You coming?" I looked behind me then headed to the dance floor.

Danny followed behind me and we danced to a few songs until I had the urge to pee.

"You okay?" Danny grabbed me as I stumbled.

"Yeah, I think those drinks are catching up to me." I grabbed my head and shook off the foggy feeling coming over me.

"Where you trying to go?"

"Bathroom."

"I got you." I felt Danny guiding me to the bathroom before I could protest. By this point, my body felt weird, almost like I was floating.

What the hell was going on?

CHAPTER 12

TARIQ

I looked around Naudia's section and realized she had been gone a while.

"Aye, where did yall say Naudia was?" I stood up and asked Renee and Trinity.

"She knew a guy at the bar and stayed to talk to him." I looked towards the bar and didn't see her.

"The bar?"

"Yeah, she's right there," Renee pointed. "Wait, where the hell did she go?" She slowly lowered her hand.

"I knew this girl was gone be on some bullshit," I mumbled.

"Aye Renee!" I turned around and some dude was walking into the section.

"Hey, Nick!" Renee walked over to him and hugged him.

"Where's my girl?" the guy asked, looking around the section, causing me to frown.

"Who's your girl?" I asked.

Renee looked at me. "Uh-"

Before Renee could lie, Brady and Lucas walked up. "Where the hell is my sister at?" Lucas asked. "And who is this nigga?" He mugged the Nick dude.

"I'm a friend a Naudia's. You know where she is?" He turned back to Renee.

My hand twitched. This must be one of the niggas she called herself fucking with.

"She was at the bar," Trinity started.

"And you fucking left her there!" Lucas walked up on her, but Brady grabbed him.

"Chill, bro."

"Naudia is an adult. She saw someone she knew and stopped to talk to him."

"So where the hell is she now?" he yelled.

"Look, fuck all that. She's got to be somewhere. Let's go look on the dance floor," I suggested.

"Yeah, yall know Naudia loves to dance."

We all separated and walked out of the section.

The place was crowded as hell and I was starting to get annoyed. "Hey, I'm about to check the bathrooms," Renee said after a few minutes.

"Ima come with you," I told her.

We headed in the direction of the bathroom.

Renee walked into the girls' bathroom and I went into the guys.

The fuck man, I thought.

Looking around the empty bathroom, my eyebrows scrunched together. It sounded like someone was groaning in pain.

I looked at the handicap stall and noticed feet up under it.

"Aye!" I knocked on the door.

It grew quiet on the other side.

I tried to push the door open, but it wouldn't budge.

"Open the damn door!" I yelled.

Seeing that the person on the other side wasn't going to answer, I stepped back, raised my foot, and sent my foot at the door.

"The fuck you doing to her?" I yelled, rushing the guy.

"Shit!" he yelled.

I grabbed him by his shirt, pulled him out the stall, and then sent my fist into his face. "You fucking hurt her!" I yelled, throwing him on the ground. I continued hitting him while he laid balled up.

Naudia groaning caused me to snap out of it. I lifted up and sent my foot down on the dude's face before rushing back into the stall. Naudia was laid out, barely conscious in the corner. Her thin ass dress was ripped, pissing me off even more.

I pulled my shirt off and gently put it on her before lifting her bridal style.

"Come on, Naudi baby!" I begged, rushing out the bathroom.

"Oh my goodness! What's wrong with her?" Renee yelled.

"Just tell everyone we got to go!" I told her, rushing towards the exit. Naudia's breathing was slow, but she was like dead weight in my arms. I prayed that nigga hadn't violated her.

My mind was racing as I stared at her.

A few seconds later, everyone came rushing out. "What the hell happened to my sister?" Lucas yelled, running up to my car.

"Man, I don't know. She was in the bathroom like this and some nigga was with her." Lucas looked at her and I could tell he was about to break down. He jumped in my backseat with her and lifted Naudia's head in his lap.

Trinity got in my front seat.

"Come on, Renee, we'll follow them," Brady said, grabbing Renee's hand.

Lucas was so focused on Naudia that he forgot he brought Alisha with him, but I didn't have time to remind him. Rushing to the driver's side. I quickly pressed my push start and drove to the hospital.

———

I SAT in the chair next to Naudia's bed with my elbows propped on my knees. She had been sleeping for the past hour. When we rushed her to the hospital, they gave her fluids, and now she was in and out of consciousness.

My jaw clenched staring at her chest rising and falling slowly. I wasn't sure what the hell happened in that bathroom, but the doctors told us she wasn't penetrated. We were currently waiting for her toxicology report to come back.

My eyes shot up when Naudia started moving. "Mhm," she mumbled.

I took a deep breath and stood up, standing over her.

"Is she waking up?" Trinity walked over to the bed and stood next to her.

She had been sitting near the window waiting for Naudia to finally wake up, Brady and Renee went off somewhere, and Lucas went to find her doctor a little bit ago.

I didn't respond, just kept my eyes on Naudia. Her eyes fluttered then slowly opened.

"Shit my head," she mumbled and reached up to grab it.

My eyebrows knitted together. I licked my lips and crossed my arms, staring down at her.

"What happened?" she asked, finally opening her eyes fully. She attempted to sit up, but Trinity stopped her.

"Hold on, I'll raise the bed," Trinity told her.

After finding the remote, she raised it so that Naudia's head was higher.

"Why am I at the hospital?" Naudia looked down at the IV in her arm, then at me and Trinity.

"I'm going to go find everyone and tell them she's up," Trinity said. "Sis, you had us nervous as hell."

Trinity left out of the room. I had yet to say anything. I was trying to keep myself calm, knowing that Naudia wasn't at her best right now. The image of her being laid out in the bathroom kept playing over in my head. The tightness I had in my chest returned briefly.

"I told you not to overdo it tonight," I finally spoke.

She balled her face up. "I didn't. What are you talking about?"

I started to chew on the inside of my jaw. "I walked in on you laid out in the damn bathroom with a nigga about to rape you!" Her eyes widened.

"Wh, wh, what?" she struggled out.

I licked my lips. "What all did you drink?"

Naudia looked down at the hospital gown she had on then back up at me. Tears were now invading her eyes. "I don't think I had anything too strong. A few shots when we went to the dance floor, nothing over the top."

She got this far away look on her face. I sighed seeing she was starting to get upset.

Stepping a little closer to the bed, I grabbed her hand. "I found you before that nigga could do anything to you. You scared the shit out me though, shit, out of everyone." Even though I was pissed, I didn't want to see her crying.

She looked up at me and gripped my hand tighter. "I don't know what happened." Bending down, I kissed her, hoping to calm her down. She lifted her hand and cuffed my face as the door opened.

I pulled away and everyone was at the door staring at us. "Lucas!" Naudia started looking nervous.

I chuckled and licked my lips. "It's cool, I already know what's up." Lucas stopped her then stepped further into the room. Naudia stared at him confused, then looked at me. I just winked at her then smirked.

"You alright, sis?" He ran his hand over her head.

Naudia slowly nodded her head. "I just don't get what happened."

"The doctor should be in here in a few."

I stepped back when Trinity and Renee rushed over to her. They were crying and apologizing for leaving her alone.

"Man, this shit's crazy," Brady said.

My eyes went back to Naudia. She had stopped crying, but I could still see the worry on her face.

"I just wish I knew who that nigga was that was in the bathroom with her." I tugged in my beard.

There was a knock on the door and the doctor walked in.

"Hi, Naudia. I'm Dr. Bloom. How are you feeling?" she asked Naudia.

"My head hurts and my mind is a little fuzzy, but besides that, I feel okay."

The doctor nodded and looked some papers over. "That's to be expected. Is it okay to talk in front of everyone?" The doctor looked around the room.

Naudia nodded. "They're all family."

"When you first came in, the gentleman here," she stopped and looked at me, "explained how he found you. We did a rape kit and it came back negative. Although that's a good thing, we did find Rohypnol in your system."

"What the hell is that?" Lucas interrupted. He was now sitting on the edge of the bed.

"It's commonly known as the date rape drug." As soon as the words left her mouth, Naudia broke down. Lucas grabbed her and pulled her into him.

"So someone drugged her?" Renee asked with her voice cracking.

Dr. Bloom nodded. "We've given you some fluids since you were highly dehydrated. Once the IV is complete and you talk to the authorities, you're free to go."

"Authorities?" I asked.

Once again, Dr. Bloom nodded. "It's standard protocol for us to call law enforcement when something like this occurs."

"My sister isn't talking to the cops," Lucas held her securely.

"Sir, it's necessary to find whoever did this."

"I, I don't remember anything. I just want to go home," Naudia cried, pulling away from his chest. I clenched my jaw. I didn't like seeing her upset.

Making my way to the bed, I sat on the side. Naudia laid her head on my chest and hugged me tightly. "Tell her I don't want to talk to anyone," she cried.

I rubbed her back and Lucas stood up. "You can see my sister isn't in the right mind to talk to anyone. It's only going to make her even more upset."

The doctor looked around the room as if someone would say anything different, but we all felt the same way. She finally sighed and allowed her shoulders to drop.

"I'll let them know. They may reach out afterwards, however." The doctor turned and walked out of the room.

"Who the fuck drugged you, Naudi?" Brady asked.

It was the first time he'd spoken since the doctor walked in.

"Yeah, what the fuck!" Lucas yelled.

He looked like he was ready for war. I didn't blame him. No matter how much he and Naudia argued, he always protected her. When their parents died, he got worse with her. She fought it, but he didn't let up.

"Who was the guy that came up to you at the bar?" Trinity asked her. I looked down at Naudia crying on my chest. She pulled up and looked at me. I could tell she was nervous to say the name, but I nodded to indicate it was okay.

"Uhm, Danny. The last thing I remember is him coming up to me offering me a drink for my birthday."

"And you drunk that shit?" Lucas yelled.

"I was right there at the bar with him. I didn't think anything of it." She sniffed back tears.

"And you just left my sister there with some random ass nigga for her to get drugged." He mugged Trinity.

"I didn't leave her! She knew the guy and we could see her from where we were sitting! Don't put this on me!" Trinity pointed her finger at him. Her face grew red.

"You shouldn't have fucking left her!"

"Lucas, it's not her fault. She's right. I knew Danny."

"Who is this nigga, Naudia?" I asked her.

She tucked her lips in her mouth.

"Answer his question!" Lucas demanded.

"Remember the guy you caught coming out of my house that day?" she said quietly.

I bit down on my lip. "So you were still dealing with that nigga?"

She quickly shook her head. "No, that was the first time I saw him since he left my house."

"See, I told yo ass to chill the hell out! You just couldn't sit the hell down somewhere," Lucas ranted.

"I didn't think this would happen."

"Look, right now all that matters is that Naudia is ok. Tariq got to her before anything bad could happen to her," Renee jumped in trying to defuse things.

"You're coming to my house," Lucas told her.

"What? No, I'm not."

"That nigga knows where you live, and you're not staying home alone."

"But I-"

"She can come to my house," I jumped in. Things grew quiet.

Naudia looked from me to Lucas. Once again, the confused look was back on her face. "Bet. I know she's safe with you."

"When did this happen?" Naudia questioned.

"Don't worry about all that. Just know he knows not to hurt you."

I chuckled and nodded. "I got her."

Things settled down, and Renee and Brady left, along with Trinity. I could tell she was more than ready to leave because of Lucas's comment; she practically ran out of here.

"Watch over my sister, Tariq. I still don't know if I'm cool with this, but I know neither of yall care." I laughed.

"Damn right." We slapped hands.

Lucas and I talked the day at the warehouse and I told him about me and Naudia. I wasn't about to hide like we were some little kids, and he was my best friend. He didn't like it when I first told him, but like he said, he knew that neither of us was going to pay it any attention. I just had enough respect to tell him what was up.

Lucas bent down and kissed Naudia's forehead. "I'll talk to you tomorrow."

He turned and headed out the room. Naudia looked up at me. "Are you going to lecture me?" she asked, getting dressed.

The IV was complete, and they had removed it from her as well as discharged her. "Nah, not right now at least. You need to rest. I just hope this is a wake-up call for you."

She looked at me with a gloomy look. "It was." She nodded.

I walked up to her and nudged myself between her legs, then bent down and kissed her. I pulled on her bottom lip with my teeth before sucking on it. "Ima get that nigga. Don't worry," I told her.

"I know." Her arms went around me, and she hugged me tightly.

For the first time since we been here, I was relaxed knowing she was safe.

CHAPTER 13

BRADY

"Are you going to tell me where we're going?" Renee looked over at me and asked.

Taking my eyes off the road for a minute, I smiled at her. "Anyone ever tell you, you're impatient as hell?"

She playfully rolled my eyes. "Well, when you just wake me up and tell me to get dressed then we get in the car, it makes me wonder."

I looked back at the road. "Just ride woman."

She smacked her lips and crossed her arms. Out the corner of my eye, I looked her over. Renee was dressed simple today, just some black leggings and a t-shirt, but she was still killing shit if you asked me. Her hair was in a bun at the top of her head and she wasn't wearing any makeup.

"Why are you being a creep?" she asked.

"How?" I smirked.

"I see you looking at me out the corner of your eye." I chuckled.

"I just like you when you're not all dressed up."

She looked down then at me. "Really? I look so basic right now."

"Nah, I think you look beautiful."

She blushed and leaned back in her seat. No more words were said between us. The radio played as I continued to drive, glancing over at Renee every once in a while.

———

"Whose house is this?" Renee asked, gripping my hand.

"You just gone keep asking questions, huh?" I grabbed my keys and found the right one to unlock the door.

"You got a secret house I never knew about?" she asked, frowning.

"Girl, come on," I laughed, pulling her into the house.

"Aye, ma!" I called out, walking deeper into the house. Renee froze.

"Ma? This is your mom's house!" I stopped and grinned.

"Yeah."

"Why didn't you tell me! I look a mess!" She snatched her hand out of mine and started messing with her hair.

"Baby, I told you, you look beautiful." I pulled her into me and kissed her temple.

"Why you come in here yelling boy?" My mom came downstairs and smiled when she saw me. "Hey baby!"

I let go of Renee and walked over to my mom, pulling her into me. "And who is this pretty young lady?" I let my mom go and looked at Renee.

"This my girl, Renee!" I held my arm out for Renee to come to me.

"Renee, this my mom, Jackie."

"Nice to meet you, Ms. Jackie!" Renee smiled.

She gave her a once over and nodded. "It's nice to meet you too, sweetheart." My mom walked over to Renee and pulled her into a hug.

"I wish you would have told when me you were on the way; I would have cooked."

"I wish he would have told me, and I would have looked more presentable." Renee cut her eyes at me.

"Baby, you look fine," I assured her.

"He's right, you're very pretty."

Renee blushed. "Thank you, ma'am."

"Come on, we can go sit on the deck," she told us.

We followed behind her to the back of the house. My mom stopped to make us something to drink before meeting us outside.

"Brady, I didn't know you were seeing someone on a serious note." My mom handed us our drinks then sat down.

I looked at Renee, who was waiting on my answer. "Yeah, well it just kind of happened." I shrugged.

"It's been a while since you brought a girl to see me. So I'm assuming you two have been dealing with each other for a while."

"Yes ma'am, a few months."

"Girl, cut all the ma'am stuff. Ms. Jackie is fine."

I stayed quiet, watching the two of them interact. My mom was nosey as hell and didn't hold back with the questions, but Renee didn't seem to mind.

"Now that you're done interrogating my girl, can we talk about why I came out here?"

Renee laughed and my mom cut her eyes at me. "I thought you came out here to see your mother?"

"I did, but you know why I really came here." My mom grew quiet and nodded.

"It's only a few days until the hearing. I sent my letter like normal, and now I just have to wait."

I stared at my mom and I could tell she was scared. "If they let him out, Brady, I know he'll kill me this time."

I clenched my fist. Getting out of my seat, I went and took a seat next to my mom. "If that nigga comes near you, I'm ending him."

I felt my blood beginning to boil. "Brady, calm down." My mom grabbed my hand. She gave it a small squeeze and smiled.

"I know I have nothing to worry about, but it still makes me nervous though." I nodded and looked at Renee, who was staring at the both of us confused.

"I didn't mean to damper the mood. I'm going to go make us something to eat." My mom patted my hand and stood up.

I rubbed the back of my neck as I watched her go into the house. Renee turned and watched her then looked at me.

"Is everything okay?" I stared at her for a minute, trying to get a grip on my emotions.

"My pops, or should I say my sperm donor, used to beat on me and my mom when I was younger. Once I got old enough to fight his ass back, he stopped. My mom finally got tired of the ass whoopings and left him. One day she called me frantic because he had found her." I stopped and thought back to that day.

Renee walked over to me and grabbed my arm. I released a deep breath. "When I got there my mom was barely conscious. He had beat her and tried to shoot her, but the cops got there before he could finish going through with it. They arrested him and sentenced him to fifteen years, but he was up for parole after ten. They've denied him the past two times, but his third hearing is coming up. My mom always gets antsy."

"Wow, I'm sorry yall went through that," I shook my head.

"It's times I feel like I'm just like that nigga. I get so pissed off and blackout."

"Don't think like that. You're a great guy and far from a monster." I gave her a lop-sided grin.

"Anyway, I doubt they let that nigga out of prison, but I wanted to make sure I came to see my mom to ease her nerves."

Renee nodded her head. "I get it. I think it's cute how you care about your mom enough to come see her."

I ran my hand over my head. "Yeah, man, that lady's my heart." I smiled.

"Aww, babe!" She moved over and kissed my face. I turned and connected my mouth with her. I pulled her into me, deepening our kiss. I moved my hand down and gripped her thigh.

"Stop before your mom comes back out here nasty," she laughed, moving away from me.

I pecked her lips again. "It's cool, I got you tonight."

We spent the rest of our day at my mom's before getting back on the road. I was glad to see her and my mom getting along.

"Make sure you both come back soon," my mom said, standing at her door.

"We will." I backed out of the driveway.

"Your mom is really nice."

"Yeah, even after the shit my dad put her through, she never turned bitter or no shit."

"She raised you to be a great person too."

"Yeah, she did, huh." Renee giggled and pulled her phone out.

I didn't share this part of my life with too many people. It was a sore subject for me. So the fact that I let her in showed me I was growing more serious about her.

CHAPTER 14

NAUDIA

The covers were snatched from over my head.

"Aye, wake up," Tariq's voice sounded from above me.

"Riq, stop playing," I groaned, reaching for the covers.

"Nah, get up. We need to talk."

I laid there with my eyes closed, hoping he would leave me alone, but it was wishful thinking.

I had been staying at Tariq's house for a week now, and for the most part, he left me alone. I was sleeping in the guest room because, for the first time in my life, I didn't feel comfortable sharing a bed with a guy. I knew Tariq wouldn't hurt me or anything but what happened to me played heavily in my head.

"Naudia, I need to talk to you on some real shit. Get up." I felt the side of the bed dip. Turning on my back, I slowly opened my eyes.

"What time is it?" I rubbed my eyes.

"Going on eleven."

"You about to head out?" I rolled on my side and stared at him.

Since being here, Tariq had been so attentive to me. He stayed home from the gambling hall the first two nights even though I assured him I was fine.

Between him and Lucas harassing me, I hadn't had time to think. I didn't want to talk about what happened to me. I wasn't raped, so I didn't see the need to discuss it further. Even the cops had tried to reach out to me once I left the hospital, but I told them I didn't know anything.

"Yeah, in a minute. I wanted to talk to you though."

"About what? It couldn't wait?"

He looked me over. "You been feeling alright since everything happened?"

I nodded. "I told you I was good."

The look on his face showed he didn't believe me. "How come you haven't been out the house then?"

I shrugged. "Just haven't felt like being bothered."

"What about school? You haven't been going to your classes." I grew quiet.

No one but Renee knew that I had been kicked out of school because I violated my probation. I didn't even think about that with everything going on.

"I talked to my professors and they've emailed me my work," I lied.

Once again, Tariq side-eyed me. He went to touch my hand and I flinched and quickly moved it away.

"See, man, you're not okay. You don't even want a nigga to touch you."

I looked down at his hand. I wasn't sure what to say. It wasn't that I didn't want him to touch me, but something in me grew nervous being so close to him now. Knowing that I was almost taken advantage of was a real wake-up call for me. With all the shit I've been through with guys, I never had one almost take advantage of me before.

"I'm sorry. I just," I stopped and sat up.

Tariq grabbed me and pulled me closer to him. "You know you can talk to me, right? You never had a problem before."

I sighed and nodded. "I know." I reached up and ran my fingers through his beard.

I wasn't really sure what was going on between us right now. Chyna hasn't been around, and I never asked if they were still together. After walking in on them, I didn't even want to be around Tariq anymore, but now he was the only person I felt completely safe around.

"Where's Chyna been?" I asked while still playing with his beard. I stared into his eyes.

"How the hell am I supposed to know that, Naudi?"

"Well, that's your girlfriend, right? Does she know I'm staying here?" A snide grin appeared on his face.

"Nah, we broke up."

My eyes widened. "Yall did? When?"

I moved my hand down from his beard and started tracing the tattoos on his neck.

"Couple weeks ago."

I squinted my eyes at him. "Why?"

He chuckled and grabbed my waist, then lifted me onto his lap.

"Because man, I'm not the type to play with girls' feelings, well not anymore. I couldn't keep stringing either of yall along. I care for Chyna, but this little hot in the ass girl put her mark on me and hasn't left my mind since."

I started blushing and lowered my head. "So now what?" I asked quietly.

Tariq gripped my chin and raised my face. His grey eyes pierced into me.

"We gone figure this shit out. When I said you needed to cut all that shit out that you were doing, I meant that. I'm not trying to be out and hear shit about my girl being out there. If we gone do this then we gone do this, ain't no half doing it or you throwing these spoiled ass tantrums when you get told something that you don't like."

I bit down on my bottom lip and processed his words. "Trust me, you don't have to worry about me being out there anymore. What happened to me taught me that I was doing too much. I was too quick to hop into bed with Danny, and it almost ended up badly because I rejected him the next time I saw him," my voice cracked.

"I should have listened to all of you when you first tried telling me I needed to calm down, but I just thought you all wanted to control and change me. I just want you to be patient with me. We all know how I can get." A small giggle left my mouth.

I swallowed hard as I waited for Tariq to answer. He moved his hand down to my neck, cuffed it securely, and pulled my face closer to his.

"I got you. We gone get that nigga too."

I told Tariq the address I had on Danny, but when he went to the house, the people who stayed there said there was no Danny there and didn't even know who it was. That confused me because I remember Danny saying that was his house when he approached me.

That was even more of a sign that I needed to relax. I didn't even know the nigga I had let in my house, in my bed.

"You better tell ole boy that keeps calling you what's up too," Tariq mentioned.

I nodded my head.

Since Nick was at the hookah bar for my birthday, he saw that something had happened to me and had been hitting me up ever since checking on me.

"I will." I puckered my lips for a kiss.

Tariq moved closer and connected his lips with mine. This

was the first time since that night I had any type of intimacy with a guy. I wrapped my arms around his neck and moved my body closer so that my breasts were pressed against his chest.

"Fuck, man, I got to go." He pulled away, panting.

I poked my lip out. "Be in my bed when I get home, alright?"

"Okay." I kissed him again. I could feel his dick starting to rise under me so I slowly grinded against it.

"You gone make me say fuck going in tonight altogether," he laughed.

I flashed him an innocent smile. "Staying here with me sounds better anyway, doesn't it?"

He gave me a once over and shook his head. "Yo ass man. Get up," I giggled and moved back on the bed. Tariq stood up and adjusted himself.

"I'll be back. Call me if you need me." I nodded my head.

He bent down and grabbed a bag off the ground. "What's this?"

"I never gave you a birthday present. I'll see you later." He bent over the bed and kissed my cheek one last time before walking out of the room.

Excitedly, I hurried and pulled the paper out of the bag and reached inside. I didn't even expect him to get me anything.

I pulled out the long box and opened it. My eyes lit up, seeing the iced-out tennis bracelet.

"Shut the fuck up," I mumbled, running my hands over the bracelet.

I looked in the bag and saw a card was inside. Grabbing the card, I opened it and read it over.

I don't even know why I'm getting your spoiled ass anything, but they say diamonds are a girl's best friend. So here's some diamonds for a diamond.

Without my permission, a smile formed on my face.

Grabbing my phone, I quickly went to Tariq's name and Face-Timed him.

He was smiling into the phone. "Thank you!" I yelled, looking at the bracelet.

"I take it you like it?"

"I love it! You know you didn't have to do this."

"Shit, I know. Do you know how much that cost?" He chuckled. "You worth it though."

The smile on my face grew. "Well, I just wanted to say thank you. I'll see you when you get home."

He grinned. "Bet." We hung the phone up and I closed the box and gripped it tightly against my chest.

Tariq seemed to amaze me more and more the more I was around him.

———

"How you feeling?" Renee asked me.

Both her and Trinity were sitting in front of me staring at me concerned.

"I'd be good if everyone stopped asking me that every two seconds," I laughed. "I'm good, yall."

They looked at each other. "What?" I stared at them curiously.

"Nothing, you just recovered quickly, I guess," Trinity shrugged.

"I mean, I still think about it from time to time, but physically I wasn't hurt. My mental is a little messed up, but I'm getting over that. I'm just pissed I got caught like that."

"We're sorry for leaving you. We should have stayed at the bar with you."

"It wasn't yall fault. I shouldn't have been so trusting with someone I had only been around twice. Trust me, lesson learned."

"I wish you would tell your brother that." Trinity rolled her eyes.

"He still giving you a hard time?" Renee asked her.

"Of course, he is. I swear his attitude is worse than mine."

I sighed. "I hate that you two are at each other's necks still. I would have thought yall would have fixed things by now."

"Hell, at this point, I don't even know if I want to fix things. Then the fact that he's already dealing with someone new makes me want to slap him every time I think about it."

"I can't believe he had the nerve to bring her to my birthday thing, knowing you would be there. I should have slapped her for you."

"Yeah, that was some fuck boy shit."

"Worse part is she's not even someone new." Trinity got this sad look on her face.

"What?"

"He's dealt with her before. Her name is Alisha. At first, I didn't recognize her because I had been drinking, but once I had a clear head, I realized that I'd had a few run-ins with her in the past."

"Wait, so he's messing with someone he's cheated on you with?" Trinity frowned at me.

"Sorry," I tossed my hands up.

"But yes, he used to creep with her here and there mostly when I would break up with him. We have had a few arguments but nothing past that. I think that's what makes it worse, knowing they have some kind of history."

"Oh, hell no, my brother is really tripping now. Why didn't you say anything?"

"I didn't want to ruin your night. Besides, Lucas and I aren't together so he's free to deal with her if he wants. Her ass is loving the attention from him. She's posted him a few times on her IG since your birthday."

My mouth dropped. Lucas was really out here wilding. He's never been this messy before. Even when he did creep on Trinity, he never gave these bitches an up on her or let them post him.

I shook my head. "So what are you going to do?"

Trinity stared at Renee with a blank expression. "Shit, nothing. I'm tired of constantly going back and forth with his ass. I loved Lucas too much, more than he loved me, obviously. I make one mistake and he completely throws in the towel with us. I'm over it."

Even though I wasn't happy about it, I had to respect it. Trinity didn't deserve how my brother was treating her.

"Okay, well if we're done eating, I need to run by the warehouse to grab something from Brady," Renee said, standing up.

Trinity looked at her like she had just lost her mind.

"Did you not just hear what I just said?"

"Girl, ain't no one thinking about Lucas. Come on." I went in my purse and pulled out a hundred-dollar bill dropping it on the table.

Trinity looked like she wanted to go against us, but she got up and followed us instead.

CHAPTER 15

TRINITY

"I DON'T THINK I'VE EVER BEEN IN HERE WHEN IT WASN'T OPEN," Renee said as we stepped into the warehouse.

"Damn, you looking good. Follow me real quick," Brady said, shutting the door. He grabbed Renee's hand and led her to the back.

"We didn't come here for yall to be nasty!" Naudia yelled out behind them.

"Mind your business," Brady laughed.

I looked around the warehouse, happy I didn't see Lucas anywhere. I was impressed with this place. I never noticed how much bigger it was compared to the old place until now.

"What you doing here?" Tariq walked up to us and stood in front of Naudia.

She smiled up at him and wrapped her arms around his neck. "Renee came to meet Brady real quick and we were with her."

Tariq looked over at me. "What's up, Trinity?"

I smiled and waved. "Hey."

"Your boy is around here somewhere," he told me, causing me to roll my eyes.

"I'm not looking for him." I waved Tariq off. That made him laugh.

"Yall two stubborn ass people." He bent down and kissed Naudia.

"Maybe if your boy would get out his feelings."

"Aye, that's your brother." Naudia and Tariq laughed.

"I'm in the middle of sorting the money for the tables. Want to join me?" Naudia looked over at me.

"I'm good, go ahead," I told her.

"You sure? You can come," Tariq said.

I shook my head. "I'm going to sit at the bar and wait. Go ahead." I waved Naudia on.

She nodded. "Okay, we won't be long. If Renee comes out before I get back, call me."

Tariq grabbed Naudia's hand and guided her towards the stairs.

I walked over to the bar and took a seat. Lucia was in school right now, so I had some free time before I had to pick her up.

I never realized how boring my life was without her and Lucas around. Today I didn't have to work so I had the day to myself. What I thought would be a girls' day quickly changed.

I was scrolling through Instagram, looking at nothing in particular, when a post from Alisha popped up. I rolled my eyes and closed the app. She had posted a picture with her straddling Lucas. He was holding her ass and she had the phone facing the mirror.

I sighed and placed my phone on the bar.

"Who let you in here?" I looked up and smacked my lips.

"Why are you talking to me?" The girl from the mall stepped behind the bar and walked to where I was.

"Does our man know you're here?" She smiled at me and started moving things around the bar.

"Our man?" I cocked my head to the side.

"Isn't that what I said? What, you thought because you have his baby that you were his only one?" she smirked.

I let off a pissed off laugh under my breath and licked my lips. Clasping my hands on the bar, I stared at her. "Look, I don't care what you and Lucas have going on. Don't bring that petty shit to me."

She smiled at me. "You right, it's not like I don't know what that dick hitting for for real."

I cut my eyes at her. "Is that right?"

"Guess we teammates now," she started laughing.

I tried to ignore it, but the girl had hit a nerve. Hearing her shamelessly brag about fucking Lucas made my blood boil. Not to mention I knew from the moment I saw her at the mall she and Lucas were fucking around.

I jumped up and grabbed the girl yanking her over the bar.

I didn't know where this strength came from, but I wasn't questioning it. The frustration I had been feeling the past few months was coming out right now.

She was yelling for me to let her go, but I ignored it and didn't let up.

"Trinity, what the fuck!" Suddenly I was yanked away, but I had a grip on the girl's hair still, so she came with me.

"Tri, let her go!" Lucas yelled, pulling on me again.

"Oh shit!" I heard from behind us and then laughing.

I finally let the girl go and she dropped to the ground. I turned around and pushed Lucas. "I knew you were fucking that bitch!" I cried.

Lucas grabbed my wrist. His jaw was clenched so tight I knew it had to be painful. His eyes were cut into slits.

"What the hell is wrong with you!" he yelled.

"Good job, sis. That hoe been asking for an ass whooping," Naudia cheered.

"Shut yo ass up." Tariq grabbed her.

"That hoe did deserve it." Lucas ignored his sister and kept his eyes on me.

"You were fucking with that hoe the whole time, huh! You made me seem like I was crazy!" I yelled, trying to snatch away from him.

"No one was fucking with that girl. How many times do I have to say that?"

"Lucas, you really gone keep this up?" the girl stood up and wiped her lip.

"Damn, sis, you did good," Naudia laughed.

"Naudia, shut the hell up!" I stared at him.

"I make one mistake and you just want to be done, but you been fucking with this bitch the whole time! How is that even fair?"

"She sucked my dick a few times, that's it. I told you it wasn't that deep with us!"

"That doesn't make it any better!"

"And you think it's cute fucking with a nigga who has a whole family at home? You're lucky he's still holding me!" I yelled.

"Chill the hell out! You're not innocent either. You fucked my nigga!"

"It was a mistake! I told you that it was one time and I didn't mean for it to happen!" He let me go and glared at me.

"It doesn't matter. You still fucked him!"

I wiped my eyes. "You know what, Lucas, fuck you! Fuck you and her. I'm over this shit." I stormed towards the door, but he grabbed me.

"Brandy, go pack your shit and get the fuck out."

"What!" she yelled.

"You're fired. I told you I don't do that messy shit. Leave." She looked at him in disbelief then turned to Tariq.

"Bitch don't look at this one," Naudia told her.

Her eyes went back to Lucas. "So because you couldn't keep your dick to yourself, I lose my job?"

"No, because you couldn't shut the hell up! Now go!" She mumbled something under her breath then stomped away.

Lucas stared down at me. "I don't have shit else to say to you." I snatched away from him.

"What did we miss?" Renee's voice sounded.

"I'll meet yall at the car," I told her and stormed to the entrance.

Lucas had completely sent me to my breaking point. I didn't have shit else to say to him outside of our daughter, and I meant that.

———

I STARED at the menu trying to figure out what I wanted to eat. I had an hour lunch break and walked down to a small deli down from the office.

My mood had been complete shit since the fiasco at Lucas's gambling hall. It had been a few days and I was still pissed off.

When I finally got to the register and decided what I wanted, I gave the lady my order. When I went to grab my wallet, someone reached around me and handed the lady a card.

"Ring hers with mine," the guy said behind me.

"I got it," I said, grabbing my card.

"It's on me, beautiful." The lady at the register took the card and smiled while ringing up the order.

"Thank you." I turned to look at the guy and took a step back.

The man in front of me was fine as hell. He had shoulder-length dreads with blond tips. He was brown-skinned with brown lips surrounded by a bushy, groomed goatee. His eyes were dark brown and currently looking me over. He was athletically built but a little on the thick side.

He smiled at me, showing a beautiful smile. "You'll really be thanking me by giving me your name."

I smiled bashfully. "Trinity."

He held his hand out. Hesitantly I grabbed his hand and he brought it to his lips and kissed it. "Myles, it's nice to meet you."

I cleared my throat and moved my hands out of his grasp.

"Nice to meet you."

My phone vibrated in my pocket. "Excuse me." I pulled it out and looked.

Rolling my eyes, I stepped to the side to answer it.

"What, Lucas?"

"Don't start that attitude shit. I'm going to get Lucia from school and keep her tonight."

"You could have texted me that."

"You know what? I'm trying to be cordial with you, Trinity."

"Whatever, Lucas. Have my baby call me before she goes to sleep." I hung the phone up and slid the phone into my pocket.

"Everything okay?" Myles asked me.

I nodded. "Just my daughters' stupid ass father," I mumbled.

They called my order out and I walked to the counter to get it.

"Well, thank you again, Myles."

"Wait, I know you not gone leave without me getting your number."

I looked around the restaurant. Even with me being mad and not officially with Lucas, I still didn't feel right giving my number out.

"Unless you have a man?" He must have noticed my face.

I shook my head. "Uhm, no, no man." I held my hand out. "I guess it's fine."

He smiled and handed his phone to me. I inserted my number and gave it back to him.

"I'll be hitting you up." I smiled and nodded.

Stepping around him, I walked out of the deli and started back to the office. The deli was close enough to walk, which I took full advantage of.

When I got to the office, Myles popped into my mind causing me to smile. He was cute and seemed nice. I just wondered if he was good enough to keep my mind off Lucas.

CHAPTER 16

LUCAS

Whoever was currently knocking on my door was about to get cursed out. Shit in my life has been stressful as fuck, and right now I just wanted a moment of peace.

We still haven't figured out who the undercover was, we hadn't found the nigga who drugged my sister, and me and Trinity have been at each other's neck more now. All I wanted to do was throw everything that annoyed me to the side for a week.

I walked to my front door and stood in front of it. "Who is it?" I asked.

"Open the door, darling brother."

I shook my head and pulled the door open.

She grinned and stepped inside the house. "Hello, big brother."

"What you doing here, Naudi?" She hasn't been my biggest fan since the shit with me and Trinity. You wouldn't even think me and her were blood-related.

"I can't come see my brother?"

I closed the door. "You haven't been fucking with me lately. Just shocked that you're here."

"You know I love you. I just don't like the decisions you've been making, but I miss you." She poked her lip.

"Shit, I been chillin," I shrugged.

She walked to my living room and sat down. "I want to sell my house." That caught me off guard.

"You do?" She nodded her head.

"Since Danny knows where I stay, I don't feel comfortable living there. Even though I been staying at Tariq's house, I know that I'll have to go home eventually."

"Speaking of, I don't like you staying with that nigga. I'm cool with yall being together, but yall too new to be living together."

"I know that," she laughed. "That's why I'm telling you I want to sell my house and get a new one. Somewhere that Danny can't get to me."

I nodded. "We can do that. I'll start looking into things."

"I knew I could count on you." I took a seat next to her.

"How you been?"

"Good, things are getting back to normal for me. I don't feel nervous about being around a lot of people anymore."

"I'm sick that nigga got that close to you with me being in the same building."

"I'm okay though."

"Yeah, but that shit still bothers me."

She grabbed my hand. "I'm fine. Nothing happened to me. It's okay."

I squeezed her hand. She could brush this off, but I wasn't. I couldn't wait to see that nigga. I didn't know what he looked like, but Tariq did.

"I have to tell you something," she finally said after a few minutes of us being quiet.

"Don't tell me you're pregnant." I mugged her.

She snatched her hand away from me and frowned. "No, fool."

Naudia took a deep breath and licked her lips. "I got kicked out of school."

"You got kicked out of school?" I felt my mouth twist upside down.

She swallowed and slowly nodded her head. "What the fuck, Naudia?"

"I didn't mean for it to happen! Some shit happened with these girls and we fought. I was on probation and ended up getting kicked out."

I glared at her. "So now what, Naudia? You know my rule, man."

She started playing with her hands. "I know, I haven't figured it out yet, but I will. I just wanted to tell you before you ask for my grades and stuff." I shook my head.

I wasn't happy hearing about her being kicked out of school. Naudia knew I had one rule, and that was for her to get her degree. It was one thing our parents wanted. I knew college wasn't for me, but Naudia was smart and used to love school. It was like she didn't like to apply herself anymore.

"Don't worry, I don't plan on just sitting on my ass. I don't know what I want to do yet, but I'll figure it out."

I didn't even say anything back. Naudia was twenty-three. At this point, I needed to get off her back and let her live her life.

"I'm not even going to yell at you. If you say you got it, then okay."

She stared at me in disbelief. "Really?"

"Yeah, you're old enough to make your own decisions."

"About time you started seeing that." I pushed her.

"Only because I see you been doing better with how you been acting."

"Speaking of. Why are you still beefing with Trinity?"

I gave her a blank stare. "Come on, man. I ain't trying to talk about that."

"But Lucas, that girl loves you. She messed up, I get it, but yall been together too long for that to end yall."

"You act like some small shit happened. I know I did my dirt, but I never slept with one of her friends or hit close to home."

Naudia smacked her lips. "What about now? You're dealing with this hoe you cheated on Trinity with. She's posting pictures of yall and everything like you weren't just engaged a few months ago."

"I don't know nothing about no pictures, but Trinity left me first. Alisha and me ain't nothing serious, we just kicking it."

"Well, yall can kick it in private because she's not invited to any group events." Naudia frowned, causing me to laugh.

"I only did that shit because I knew it would piss Trinity off. That was childish, huh?"

"As hell."

I chuckled again. "You're my brother, and just like you wanted the best for me, I want the best for you. Don't ruin a good thing because your pride is hurt, big brother. Once a girl stops caring for real, you can't get her back. If she moves on, I don't want any shit from you."

I stared at her. "When the hell you get so logical?"

"I have always been logical, big brother. Yall just never paid me any attention." She smiled and stood up.

"Now, where is my niece at? I want to spend some time with her."

"She was in her room watching TV." Naudia nodded and headed towards the stairs while I sat there playing her words over.

Even if I didn't want to hear what she was saying, she was telling the truth. I did a lot of shit to Trinity, but I wasn't sure if I could overlook her doing something like this. Not to mention if she moved on, I knew I wouldn't take that lightly either.

Naudia and Lucia came into view a few minutes later while I was still in deep thought.

"Daddy, I'm going with TT!" Lucia ran up to me.

I smiled at Lucia.

Even with the stuff going on between me and her mom, she was always smiling and happy. I hated my baby girl was going through all this, but she seemed to be adapting to it now.

"Be good for TT, okay?"

She nodded.

"I will." Leaning forward, Lucia kissed my cheek then ran over to Naudia.

"Think about what I said, Lucas," Naudia said, grabbing Lucia's hand to leave.

As if she knew my sister was talking about her, Alisha was FaceTiming me.

"Hey!" She smiled into the camera.

I stared at her, noticing she was only in her bra and panties.

"What's up?" I asked, reaching over to the ashtray on the side of me and grabbing my blunt.

"Are you busy?"

"I'm about to head to the warehouse in a minute. You need something?"

She frowned. "You can't push that back to spend some time with me? I wanted to go to the mall."

I grabbed my lighter and lit my blunt. "You gone pay my bills?" I blew the smoke out and waited for her to answer.

She rolled her eyes. "Don't play with me." Stopping her giggle, she licked her lips.

"If we can't go shopping, then how about we meet up for something else?"

Alisha raised her phone above her head, giving me an overview. My dick got hard, seeing she was just in her bra and panties.

I pulled from my blunt again and smirked.

"Where you at?"

"At home, you coming?"

Since Naudia had Lucia, I didn't have shit to do until I went to the gambling hall.

"Yeah, I'll be there in a minute. I need to talk to you too."

"Okay." She smiled and hung up.

I shook my head and leaned it back on the couch, finishing up my blunt.

———

"Took you long enough." Alisha wrapped her arms around my neck and jumped onto me.

I kicked her door closed and gripped her ass cheeks.

"I been wanting to feel you all day," she moaned, grinding against me. She moved forward and kissed me while I walked to her room.

When we got in her room, I threw her on her bed and got on top of her.

I kissed her neck then down to her chest. I took one out of the bra and kissed the top before getting to her nipple.

"Lucas, you don't know how much I missed you. How much I missed this." She reached for my waistband.

I raised up and chuckled.

Pulling my shirt over my head, I undid my pants and grabbed the condom out of my pocket before stroking my dick.

"You missed this dick, huh?" I asked, looking down at her.

She nodded and sat up. Moving forward, she smacked my hand away and took my dick in her mouth.

Alisha moved her hand up and down, circling my pole.

I grabbed her head and pushed my dick further down her throat.

"Stop being a baby and deep throat my shit," I growled, throwing my hips against her face.

She started slurping and making her head sloppier.

She tried to deep throat me but gagged. Eventually I came and she pulled away from me.

"You too old not to know how to suck dick," I mumbled, shaking my head.

I grabbed the condom and secured it on my dick after stroking my dick back to life.

"I hadn't had one that size in a while," she bit down on her bottom lip and spread her legs.

I didn't comment back. Alisha's head might not be all that, but her pussy was always good.

I grabbed her legs and pushed them forward so they were near her head. Placing my dick at her entrance, I pushed into her.

"Fuck, I needed this," she moaned.

I started moving in and out of her. Alisha's pussy held a mean grip on my dick, and it seemed like she kept gripping it tighter.

Alisha started playing with her nipples with her eyes closed.

"You always had some good pussy," I groaned, pulling out of her.

"Turn around." She flipped over on all fours and put a perfect arch in her back.

I grabbed her hips and pushed inside her. Soon as I entered her, Alisha started throwing her ass to match my stroke.

After going at it for a few rounds, we both were cumming.

I slowly pulled out of her, making sure the condom was still intact, and stood up.

After going to the bathroom to flush the condom and wash my dick off, I walked back into her room. She slid over and onto my lap.

"Why you seem stressed, baby?" She kissed on my neck.

I grabbed her thigh and gripped it.

"You posting pictures of us on social media?" I asked her.

She looked at me, smiling innocently at me. "I mean, I posted some. So," she shrugged.

I frowned. "Chill out on that." Her eyebrows bunched together.

"Why?"

"Me and my baby mom just separated. I don't need any drama with her. Let shit settle first."

She rolled her eyes. "If yall not together, then I don't see why it matters."

"It matters because I ain't trying to beef with my daughter's mother. Just don't be posting me, alright?"

She rolled her eyes but nodded. "I guess because it's for your daughter, I can listen."

I laughed. "Nah, you gone listen because I told you to." She leaned forward and pecked my lips.

"You right." She pulled away and stared at me.

"I been wanting this with us for a while, but you always been with Trinity."

"Oh yeah." I ran my hand up and down her bare thigh.

"Yeah, hopefully, we can make something work." She smiled widely.

"Shit, a nigga just got out of a relationship. You want me back in one already?"

She giggled. "I'm not saying right now. I'm just throwing it out there. You know how I felt about you back then."

"Nah, I know how you felt about a nigga's pockets." She smacked her lips.

"I told you I ain't even like that anymore."

"Yeah alright. Look, I need to head home and shower. I'll hit you up later."

She pouted but nodded.

Once she was off of me, I started getting dressed to leave. I checked my phone and saw Naudia said she had talked to Trinity and she was keeping Lucia for the night.

I frowned.

"Bye!" Alisha said behind me.

Once I got in my car, I dialed Trinity.

"What, Lucas?"

"Why ain't you call me to tell me Naudia was keeping Lucia?"

"Seriously? That's why you called me?"

"Hell yeah, I should have been told."

"Whatever, Lucas. She told you, so you know. I'm busy."

"Doing what?"

"Bye." She hung up the phone and I chuckled.

The last few times I talked to Trinity, her mouth was slick as hell. I wasn't going to keep dealing with it.

CHAPTER 17

TARIQ

I WRAPPED MY ARMS AROUND NAUDIA AND PULLED HER INTO ME. I kissed on the back of her neck and moved my hand down her stomach until I got to her panty line.

"What are you doing?" she moaned.

I sucked on the back of her neck and slipped my hand into her panties. "Open up."

This would be the first time we'd be intimate since everything happened on her birthday.

"You know how hard it is having you in my bed and not touch you." I positioned her on her back then got on top of her.

I kissed her lips and used my knee to pry her legs open. "Mhm, I missed you too." Her arms went around my neck.

I kissed down her face, and soon as I got to her neck, there was a knock on the door.

I dug my face into her neck and groaned. "TT!" Lucia knocked, opening the door.

I quickly moved over and laid on my back. Seeing that my dick didn't get the memo, I quickly grabbed a pillow and threw it over me.

"Uncle Riq?" she asked.

I sat up and smiled.

"What's up, pretty girl."

"Lucia, did we say to come in?" Naudia asked her.

Lucia looked at her confused. "But I knocked."

I chuckled and Naudia shook her head. "Let me throw some clothes on. I'll be out."

"Why are you in the bed with Uncle Riq?" She looked between the two of us.

"Little girl, go." Naudia pointed at the door, causing her to laugh.

"You picked the perfect day to keep her," I laughed and leaned over to kiss her cheek.

"I know, I should have taken her ass home."

Naudia climbed out of bed and headed into the bathroom with me behind her.

After both of us handled our hygiene and got dressed, we went downstairs where Lucia was looking at her *iPad*.

"You hungry?" Naudia asked her.

Lucia jumped and nodded.

They headed to the kitchen while I looked towards my door. I heard it open and knew it could only be one person.

"Shit," I looked towards the direction of the kitchen.

I headed towards the door and Chyna was standing there. I stared at her while she stared at me.

Damn, she looked good as hell, I thought.

"What's up Chyna? What you doing here?" I asked her, crossing my arms.

She smiled at me. "It's been a while since I've seen you. I know you said you needed time, but I missed you." She walked up to me, and her smile seemed to grow.

I stared at her sensing a sense of calmness surrounding her. Her energy was much different from the last time I saw her.

"Why you just standing there like you don't miss me? We

need to quit this stupid break and fix our shit." She stopped and stared at me with a raised eyebrow.

"Chyna, look," I paused and looked her over again. I squinted my eyes trying to see what else seemed off about her.

"Riq, do you want pancakes?" Naudia called out, approaching us.

The smile and Chyna's face slowly faded. "So you really moved on with this bitch?" Chyna snapped. The calmness she just had was gone that fast.

Naudia came and stood next to me. She popped her hip to the side and placed her hand on it. "Didn't that bitch word get you fucked up last time?"

Chyna ignored her and looked at me. "So all that time you said I was crazy, I really wasn't, huh? You really left me for her? A bitch that's been passed around more than a damn basketball."

I grabbed Naudia just as she went to charge at Chyna. "Go in the kitchen with Lucia, and I'll handle this," I said in her ear.

I could feel her tense up in my arms. My eyes went to Chyna and I could see the hurt displayed on her face.

Naudia pulled away from me then turned and glared at me. "Hurry up." She leaned up and kissed me. Pulling away, she turned and looked at Chyna one last time before walking back towards the kitchen.

I blew a deep breath out and looked at Chyna. Now she looked like she was about to break down.

"Chyna, listen, man."

"Seriously, Tariq! Two years and that's how you do me!" She looked in the direction Naudia had just gone.

"You know I never wanted to hurt you. That's why I told you we needed to take a break. Shit with me and Naudia just kind of flows." I stared at her. It fucked me up that once again, I was causing her to cry.

"So that's it? Me and you are done?"

"Chyna, come on, don't make this hard."

"I thought you loved me. Did you lie when you said that?"

I tugged on my beard. "You know I didn't lie about that shit. I do love you, Chyna. I just- Fuck, look, shit is hard to explain. Maybe it's because we grew up together, but my feelings for Naudia are something I can't fight anymore. I tried to; I didn't want to do you like that, but it just happened."

If looks could kill, I'd be dead. Chyna licked her lips then nodded. Grabbing her key ring, she played with it for a minute before I heard something hit the ground. I looked down and saw it was my key.

"I hope when she fucks you over you don't come looking for me." Turning around, she exited my house.

I sighed and shook my head.

Turning around, I walked to my kitchen.

Lucia was sitting at the table in the corner. Just like the living room, the kitchen was an open floor plan too.

I walked over to where Naudia was and wrapped my arms around her waist. "Did you handle that?" She turned around to face me.

"I told you I would, right?" I pulled her into me.

"Good because I would hate to have to beat her ass again." I chuckled.

"You ain't going to do shit." I leaned down and kissed her.

"Eww!" Lucia yelled from across the kitchen. I pulled away from Naudia, who snickered.

"You nosey as hell, Lucia." I turned and walked over to her.

She laughed and looked back at the *iPad*. I took a seat next to her and pulled my phone out and saw Brady calling me.

"What's up?"

"Meet us at the hall," he said then hung up.

I stared at the phone curiously.

"Aye, I have to go meet up with your brother and Brady," I

said, standing up. "I'll see you later, Lucia." I ran my hand over her head then walked over to Naudia.

Her phone was going off on the counter. "Handle that nigga before I have to," I told her, noticing the Nick dude was calling.

She turned around to speak, but I silenced her with a kiss. I didn't want any excuses. I just wanted her to handle it.

———

"So what's up?" I asked, walking into the office at the hall.

"Remember Vicky's baby daddy?" Brady asked.

I nodded and leaned on the wall. "What about him?"

"We got to handle that nigga," Lucas said, sitting up in his chair.

"What happened?" I looked between the two.

"That nigga been talking greasy since we beat his ass and kicked him out."

"Yall think it's something we should be worried about?"

"Shit, it's not something I want to find out," Lucas replied.

"Yeah, we should have been dealt with that nigga. There was no way he was going to take that ass whooping laying down."

"Shit, yall right. So when yall want to handle this?"

"I'm getting information about him now. We can move in on him this weekend," Brady announced.

"I'm with it. The sooner the better."

Pushing myself off the wall, I thought about all the extra shit that's been thrown our way. "Man, it's like we get hit with one thing after another."

"I was just thinking that shit. Niggas can never make money in peace."

"Aye, speaking of peace. Yo cock blocking ass daughter ruined my shit earlier," I mugged Lucas.

He laughed. "What she do?"

"I was lying in bed with Naudia and her ass came busting in the room."

Lucas stopped laughing and mugged me. "Good, that's what her ass was supposed to do."

Shaking my head, I smirked. "It's cool, she going back to Trinity tonight."

I chuckled and Brady joined in.

"Fuck you, nigga."

"I got some more pills in too," Brady mentioned reaching for the bag on the side of him.

Since we all were here, we decided to start getting set up for tonight. First, we separated the pills, then I started preparing the money while Lucas and Brady went to the floor.

CHAPTER 18

RENEE

I sighed in relief staring at my laptop. I was looking at my final grades for school and passed every class. Now I had the summer off until the fall.

This semester was rough. With me getting closer to graduating, I wasn't shocked, but it would all be worth it once I finished.

Since I was in a good mood, I wanted to go out and celebrate.

Looking around for my phone, I grabbed it then started a group Facetime with Trinity and Naudia.

"Hey hoes!" I said once both of them answered.

"You're in a good mood," Trinity noted.

"Yeah, what's up?"

I smiled widely. "I got my final grades back from school and I passed. Let's go out and celebrate."

"Aww shit, that's what's up!" Naudia cheered.

"Yeah, good job, Nae!"

"So, do you heffas want to go out?"

"I don't see why not. Let me see if my parents will keep Lucia. If so, I'm down."

I noticed Naudia hadn't said anything. I stared at the screen and saw she looked worried. "Everything okay?"

"I just don't know if I want to go out, that's all," I frowned.

"Since when?"

She licked her lips. "Since my birthday. I don't really feel comfortable about being in a crowded setting."

I stopped and thought about it. It did make sense for Naudia to be anxious after what she went through, especially since this Danny dude seemed to have vanished into thin air.

"How about we go to the guys' gambling hall? We can chill in the sitting area. We know that no one is going to mess with you at your brother's place of business."

"Count me out. I don't want to be near my child's father." Trinity rolled her eyes.

"Girl bye, you miss my brother. Yall both just playing," Naudia laughed.

Trinity smacked her lips. "Whatever, let me know what time to be ready, and one of yall is coming to get me."

"I don't plan on drinking, so I'll be the driver tonight," Naudia offered, shocking me.

"Damn, sis. You sure you good?" Naudia snickered.

"Yes, just cutting back. I'll see yall at eleven."

Since I had some time to kill, I decided to go get pampered. Today was a celebration, so I wanted to show out.

———

NAUDIA, Trinity, and I walked into the gambling hall like we owned the place, and it seemed like all eyes were on us.

"Do the guys know you're here?" the bouncer asked us.

I looked at the girls and Naudia smiled at him. "Why do we have to go through this every time we walk in here?"

"Because you know how your brother feels about you being here."

Naudia ran her finger down his chest and smiled. "And yet you always allow me back in." She winked at him.

Trinity and I looked at each other and laughed before we all walked further into the hall.

"Girl, you better stop flirting with that nigga unless you want Tariq to fuck you up," Trinity laughed.

"They always try to give me a hard time coming in here. He likes me so I use that to my advantage." Naudia shrugged and looked around.

I could see the tense look on her face. "You're cool with being here, right?" I touched her shoulder and she jumped. We made eye contact and she forced a smile on her face.

"Yeah, I'm good." She looked around the warehouse.

"Let's grab a drink, then we can go play a table or something," Trinity suggested.

Naudia nodded. "I'm down."

We headed for the bar. While Trinity and I ordered drinks, Naudia stood to the side, observing the crowd. "You come to my place of business and not tell me." I smiled, hearing his voice behind me.

Brady's arms wrapped around me and he kissed the back of my neck. "I'm here celebrating." I smiled and turned around to face him. My arms went around his neck and I leaned up to kiss him.

"We're going to the tables, Renee!" Naudia said. She and Trinity waved at Brady. He sent them a head nod, and they walked away.

"What are you celebrating?" Brady raised an eyebrow.

A wide grin forced its way on my face. "I passed all my classes with flying colors."

"Why didn't yo ass tell me? I would have taken you out." He pulled me into him and kissed me. Hugging me tightly, our kiss deepened.

"I knew you were busy," I mumbled against his mouth.

"Fuck that, you should have told me. I'm proud of you, baby." His hands went to my ass and he squeezed it.

"Cherie! Whatever drinks my lady orders are on the house," Brady told the girl behind the bar. She looked from me to Brady and plastered a fake smile on her face.

"Of course, boss." She rolled her eyes and went back to making the drink she was working on.

I was in such a good mood I didn't even want to check her.

"I love that you take school seriously. That shit sexy as hell, baby." He pecked my lips.

"Thank you. I'm just glad I have a few months off to relax." Brady let me go and grabbed my hand.

"I'll let you go kick it with your girls, but we are celebrating tomorrow." He walked me to the table where Trinity and Naudia were playing.

"You're not drinking, sis?" he asked Naudia.

She shook her head. "Cutting back, you know." She gave him a weak smile.

"I got some things to look over but leave with me tonight," Brady said into my ear. He hugged my waist securely.

I turned to look at him. "Let me make sure I have a lot of liquor in me in that case." I bit down on my bottom lip.

He chuckled and let me go. "You trying to start something I see."

Brady turned and walked away from us. I turned to face the girls and they smiled. "You two are so cute," Trinity gushed.

I playfully rolled my eyes. "Stop," I giggled, blushing.

The three of us continued to play and drink; well, Naudia just played the tables. I was actually having a good time celebrating. We ended up going to sit in the chill area the guys had set up. We were laughing and talking amongst ourselves after leaving the tables.

"Oh shit," Naudia suddenly mumbled.

"What's wrong?" We all looked up then our eyes went to Trinity. She looked up and smacked her lips.

Grabbing her drink, she took a sip, looking uninterested.

"Who told yo pretty ass to come in here and not let me know?" Tariq took a seat next to Naudia and grabbed her chin, pecking her lips. She blushed and poked her lips out.

"I'm surprised it took you this long to notice," she told him.

The two of them got lost in each other, talking quietly among themselves.

"What's up, Renee. Brady told us about your classes. Congrats," Lucas said.

I smiled up at him. "Thanks, bro."

His attention went to Trinity. She continued drinking as if he was standing over her.

"So you come to my place and don't speak?"

Trinity looked at him and rolled her eyes. "Hello, Lucas." He smirked.

His attention went to Naudia and Tariq and a frown appeared on his face. "I see you not turned up tonight," he told her.

Naudia took her attention off Tariq and looked at him. "I'm taking a step back from drinking, ole darling brother."

Lucas nodded.

The guys went back to working the floor after talking to us for a while. The night began to wind down. While the guys started to clear the place out, the three of us stayed in the chill area talking until they were finished.

CHAPTER 19

NAUDIA

"I don't remember the last time I saw you this lit," I laughed, holding Trinity.

She gave me a chinky eyed grin. "I haven't felt like this in a while," she laughed.

"I'm glad you enjoyed yourself," Renee laughed.

Brady walked up to Renee and grabbed her. "You ready, baby!" Renee looked at him and nodded, biting down on her bottom lip.

"You need help getting her to the car," Renee asked me.

I looked over at Trinity, who was smiling in her phone.

"No, go ahead. I got her."

"Okay, let me know when yall get home." She waved to us, and she and Brady walked off.

"Come on, drunkie," I laughed.

I grabbed her and started to pull on her, but Tariq and Lucas stopped us. "So I guess yall done switched roles, huh?" Lucas looked at Trinity frowning.

She laughed on the side of me. "Lucas, leave the girl alone," I told him.

"You gone drop her off then head to the crib?" Tariq looked down at me.

The way his gray eyes stared at me caused me to squirm. It had been a while since I had sex, I was finally feeling comfortable enough to be touched. Tariq had been patient with me, and I couldn't wait to feel him again.

"Yeah, straight home," I said lowly, gazing into his eyes.

"I know that look, Naudi! You want some dick. I can take an Uber and you can go with your man," Trinity laughed.

I giggled then looked at Tariq, who smirked.

"I don't want to hear that shit!" Lucas complained.

"You complain too much," Trinity commented.

I looked at Lucas and his scowl deepened. I knew it was time to get Trinity out of here.

"Okay, sis, come on. Let's go," I went to help her walk, but she stumbled.

"You're too fucking drunk, Trinity! You know you can't handle your liquor!"

"So what, Lucas. I'm not your responsibility anymore. Plus, I'm grown. I can do what I want," she giggled.

"Looking at how you're acting shows that's a not good thing." He curled his lip up.

She rolled her eyes. "I'm glad I moved on from your stupid ass!"

"Moved on? Who the fuck you think you moving on with, Tri?" He stepped up to her.

Trinity snatched away from me. "Don't worry about it, just know my baby is about to have a stepdaddy," she grinned.

My eyes widened.

Lucas ran his hand over his head and chuckled. He ran his tongue over his bottom lip. "I ain't even going to play with you. You know better than to try some slick shit like that, but then again, who knows? You didn't know not to hop on my homeboy's dick."

"Lucas!"

"Alright, bro, that's enough." Tariq grabbed him.

"Well, maybe if you weren't sticking your dick into bitches like Alisha, I would have never slept with him!" Trinity yelled.

"I swear if you wasn't my daughter's mom-"

"Then what?" Trinity wasn't backing down.

Lucas stared down at Trinity. I could tell he was trying to keep calm. "Naudia, you can go straight home. I got Trinity." I shook my head.

"No Lucas, I got her."

"I said I got her." His eyes didn't leave hers.

"I'm not going anywhere with you." She went to walk off, but he snatched her up and tossed her over his shoulder, causing her to squeal.

"Lucas, put me down."

Lucas ignored her and continued towards the door. I shook my head and laughed.

"They just need to make up," I said.

Tariq looked in their direction then back at me. "They'll work they shit out, but for now, I got something you need to work out."

I stared at him confused. "What?"

He grabbed my hand and placed it on his dick. I bit down on my bottom lip. "I think I can help with that." Gripping my hand, he pulled me towards the door with me giggling behind him.

As soon as Tariq and I parked our cars and got into his house, we were on each other. He carried me to his room and dropped me on the bed, instantly stripping me out of my clothes and climbing between my legs.

"Shit, it's been so long," I moaned, clawing at Tariq's back.

He pulled his face away from my neck and stared down at me. "I've been missing you, missing this." He pushed deep inside me, causing my grip on him to tighten.

Tariq bent down and connected his mouth with mine. His tongue invaded my mouth and his stroke deepened.

I started moving my hips against his. "That's right, baby, throw that pussy at me." He pulled up and grabbed my legs. He held them in his hand and circled his hips into me.

"Tariq, slow down." I reached up and attempted to push him away.

"Nah, don't tell me you can't take the dick anymore." I licked my lips and sat up some, staring at his dick moving in and out of me.

Tariq let go of my legs and bent down, taking my exposed nipple in his mouth. He bit down on it and ran his tongue over it.

"Tariq," I moaned, clenching my pussy together. He started kissing up my chest until he got to my neck. He sucked and bit down on it. My body started shaking and then I was cumming.

"Shit!" Tariq groaned, pulling up and looking down.

He pulled his dick out of me then moved down. His mouth covered my pussy, licking my juices. I felt him spread my pussy lips and he pulled on my sensitive clit.

"Baby!" I cried, grabbing his head.

Tariq stuck his tongue in me and started thumbing on my clit. My eyes rolled to the back of my head. I attempted to push his head back, but he grabbed my thighs and pulled his face closer to me.

Soon I was cumming in his mouth. He continued to suck on my pussy for a few more seconds before pulling up.

I lazily stared at him as his beard shined with my juices.

"Tariq, I don't think I can take anymore," I complained.

He smirked and rubbed on my clit, causing my leg to twitch.

"You not tapping on me, Naudi!" He laid on his back, grabbed me, then pulled me on top of him.

"Riq!" I whined.

He ignored me and guided me down on his pole. I gripped his sweaty chest and started rocking my hips. His strong hands played with my breasts, massaging my nipples. I started bouncing my ass up and down.

Tariq stared at me lustfully. He tucked his bottom lip between his teeth. His eyes narrowed and he pinched my nipples.

One of his hands moved down and went back to my clit. "I'm so happy we made this official," I told him, staring down at him.

Tariq's eyes met mine. "Shit, me too. You're the shit, Naudia." I felt his dick jerking inside me, so I knew he was close to cumming.

I started rocking my hips faster and gripped his dick with my pussy. My stomach grew tight. Tariq leaned up and held me. He started fucking me from below, and before long, we were cumming together.

I laid on him and grabbed his face while we engaged in a passionate kiss. My body felt like it was floating. Tariq made me feel things I had never felt before. He made me feel loved, like I was special.

"I'm serious about me being happy that we got together, Riq," I told him once we were all cleaned up and lying in bed. I had one of my legs over his body and my hands were running through his beard. "I know that us being together at first wasn't ideal. In fact, it was wrong, but I don't regret it."

"Shit, me neither. You're special, Naudia. You're loyal, and you keep a nigga on his toes," he stopped and laughed. "But more importantly, you've grown so much in these past few months. I love the woman your becoming and I'm glad you're in my life for me to watch you transform into that woman."

I lifted up and stared at him. He moved his hand up and cuffed my cheek. I bent down and kissed him. He pulled me down on him and held me tightly.

Tariq lit something in me I never felt before. I hoped the way I was feeling never went away.

———

"So your house is sold," Lucas told me when I stepped into his house.

I smiled widely and nodded. That was a relief. I wasn't trying to go back to my old house. Knowing that Danny knew where I stayed made me nervous. I had only been to my house to grab clothes, but it was never alone.

"So what's next?" I asked him.

"You get the money from the house and then we look for you another place." I slowly nodded.

I wasn't sure how I felt about that. I actually liked staying with Tariq. He didn't complain about me being there either.

"So when do you want to do that?" I looked at him.

"I'll talk to the real estate agent and have her line up some houses to show and we'll go from there."

I sighed and nodded once again. "What's wrong?"

"I just hate I have to leave my house because I was stupid and careless. I should have listened to you." I closed my eyes and covered my face with my hands.

Sometimes the night of my birthday seemed to come to me in pieces, or at least it felt like it did. I would be asleep and then Danny's face would appear over me, touching and kissing on me. When I tried to push him away, my body would be stuck, unable to move.

I jumped when I felt Lucas wrap his arms around me. He pulled me into his side and held me there. "Stop thinking about that shit. As long as you know now, it's all good. That nigga isn't getting away with this." I opened my eyes.

"Yeah, I know. So what happened last night?" I asked him, trying to shift the subject.

He looked down at me. "What you mean?"

"With Trinity. What happened after you took her home?"

"Shit, nothing. She cursed me out half the way to her house then fell asleep. I took her home, helped her inside, and left."

"I thought you hated her. Why did you want to take her home?"

"Man, I could never hate Tri. I hate what she did, but I could never hate her. I just felt like it was my responsibility to get her home safe. At the end of the day, she's Lucia's mom. I guess I'm used to being that protector for her." He let me go and I stared at him.

"Lucas, it's obvious you miss her. Why not fix things with her?"

"Nah, I'm cool on that." He shook his head.

"Okay, but when her words from last night become true, then what?"

He mugged me. "Anyway, I'll tell the agent we want to see the houses by the end of the week." I smirked and nodded.

Standing up, I grabbed his hand to get him to stand. "Thank you for always looking out for me. I know sometimes I can be a spoiled brat, but you took over raising me when mom and dad died, and you didn't have to. I'm thankful to have a brother like you." I hugged him tightly.

Lucas hugged me and kissed the top of my head. "You know it's you and me until the wheels fall off, sis." I smiled and let him go.

I turned and started towards the door. When I opened it, the Alisha girl was on the other side about to knock.

"She knows where you live?" I frowned, looking back at my brother.

"Bye, Naudia." He walked over to me and held the door.

Alisha stared at me with a snide look on her face. I looked her up and down then back at Lucas. "You're really downgrading from my sister with her just to let you know." I walked out the door, making sure to bump shoulders with Alisha.

"Little girl, don't get an ass whooping you can't handle."

Pausing, I turned to look at her. "Trust me, it won't be from you." I looked at Lucas and shook my head.

I heard him fussing at Alisha and she said something back, but I continued to my car.

Just like I used to want Lucas to stay out of my business, I was going to stay out of his.

CHAPTER 20

TRINITY

"When you gone, let me take you out?" Myles asked through the phone.

I looked at the camera before focusing back on the mirror. "How many times do I have to tell you I'm not looking to date right now," I grinned, running the straightener through my hair.

"So that means you can't have a drink with a friend?" I giggled.

"I guess a drink isn't anything bad."

"What about this Friday?"

I stopped straightening my hair and looked back at the camera. "Friday is good. Just let me know the time and location."

"Mommy, I'm ready!" Lucia ran into the room.

"I'll do that, beautiful," he said.

"Is that my daddy!" Lucia yelled, rushing towards the phone.

"No, Lucia." Before I could stop her, she was grabbing the phone.

"Hey, pretty girl."

Lucia frowned and looked up at me. "Who are you?" she asked.

"That's mommy's friend." I sat the straightener on my counter.

"Go watch TV while I finish my hair and then we can go," I said, grabbing the phone.

She looked at the phone again one last time, then nodded and ran out the bathroom.

I took a deep breath and shook my head. "Sorry about that. I need to finish getting ready. I'll talk to you later, okay," I told him.

He stared at the screen curiously. "Are you okay?"

I looked at my door then back at the phone. "Yeah, I'm fine."

"Alright, I'll see you Friday then." I gave him a soft smile.

"Okay, bye." I quickly hung the phone up and looked in the mirror. It felt weird that Lucia saw me on the phone with someone who wasn't Lucas. It was a harmless conversation, but I felt that she shouldn't have seen me talking to another man.

I finished my hair up then went and got dressed.

"Lucia, are you ready?" I walked into the living room and saw she was watching TV.

She turned to look at me and nodded. Lucia turned off the TV and ran to me. I looked her over, nodding in approval at the dress she had put on.

"Who were you talking to, mommy?" she asked as we headed out the door.

I looked down at her. It was scary how much she looked like Lucas and Naudia.

"Just a friend."

"Does daddy know him?"

I swallowed hard. "No, daddy doesn't."

She furrowed her eyebrows together. I couldn't stop the laugh that escaped my mouth. Now she really looked like Lucas.

"Where we going first?" I asked her once we were in the car.

"Movies!" she yelled.

I nodded then backed out my driveway.

Today I promised her a mommy and daughter day, so the movies it was.

———

"D͏ID YOU HAVE FUN TODAY?" I held Lucia's hand as we walked out of the mall to the car.

"Yep, I can't wait to play with my new bear!" she gushed, gripping the *Build-A-Bear* I had just gotten her in her other hand.

I giggled. I loved seeing Lucia happy. It made all the madness in my life worth it just to see her smiling.

"So now let's go get some food and snacks, then we can end the night laying on the couch watching more movies," I told her.

"Okay!"

We got to my car but stopped when I heard my name being called. "Trinity, hold on."

I looked over my shoulder and my heart started beating faster.

"Lucia, get in the car," I told her, hitting the button on my keys.

"Who is that, mommy?" she asked, looking around me. I shielded her and opened the back door.

"Get in the car now!" I damn near shouted, causing her to jump. She looked at me worried.

"Baby, just get in the car."

"Trinity, it's nice to see you again. Is that your daughter?" Soon as Lucia was in the car, I slammed the door and stood in front of it. I turned and glared at Trevor.

"What do you want, Trevor?"

He smiled at me, causing a chill to shoot through me. "I like your hair like this." He went to touch my hair, but I snatched it away from his grasp.

"Don't touch me." I turned my mouth up.

He licked his lips and looked me over. "Why you acting like that, Trinity? You know I've always cared about you."

"You ruined my fucking relationship!"

"Fuck your relationship. That nigga didn't even deserve you."

"So what! What we did was wrong. You were his friend."

"It doesn't matter. I wanted you first and he knew that."

"Just leave me alone, Trevor. I don't want any more issues with you." I turned around to open my door, but he grabbed my arm.

"Let me take you out?" I looked down at his hand disgusted before snatching my arm away from him.

"Are you fucking crazy! Lucas would kill both of us. I don't see you like that, Trevor. We were a mistake."

His eyes grew dark. "What if I take Lucas out, then you'll go out with me?"

"Take him out?" I balled my face up.

He licked his lips then smiled. His eyes went to my back seat, so I shifted over so he couldn't see my daughter.

"Him and the boys seem to be doing really well. Sucks I missed out on that." He rubbed his chin. "I was around when they used to gamble back in the day, but I never thought they would be this big."

I wasn't sure where he was going with this. "Our main problem is Lucas, right? He goes away, and then we can be together?"

"What, no. I don't want you, Trevor! Even if Lucas wasn't around." He laughed.

"Yeah, alright. I still remember your moans from that night. It didn't sound that way to me."

"Like I said that night was a mistake. Now if you'll excuse me." He backed away and nodded.

"You look nice by the way." I got in my car and slammed the door, hurrying to lock the door.

"Mommy, was that another one of your friends?" Trevor was still standing next to my car, smiling.

"That's one of daddy's old friends. Buckle up," I told her, starting the car and hurrying out the parking lot.

I looked in my rearview mirror and Trevor was still standing there staring at my car. I swallowed hard and took a few deep breaths trying to slow down my racing heart. It was obvious Trevor wasn't going to go away, and I needed to tell Lucas ASAP.

———

I HELD Lucia's hand and went to knock on Lucas's door before remembering I had a key. "I didn't know we were coming to see daddy!" Lucia said.

I looked down at her and opened the door.

"Daddy!" Lucia yelled as we walked into the house. "Daddy!"

She went running towards the stairs, but Lucas was already meeting her halfway.

She ran to him and jumped in his arms. "What's up, baby!" He smiled and kissed all over her face.

Looking up from her, he stared at me. "What yall doing here?"

"I need to talk to you," I informed him, wrapping my arms around myself.

"Lucas, I'll call you later!" My eyes went behind him, and I had to contain myself seeing Alisha walking down the stairs. Her hair looked sweated out and her clothes like they were rushed on. I looked at Lucas and noticed he was only in some basketball shorts.

I squinted my eyes.

Lucia being the nosey child she was, looked at Alisha. "Who is that daddy? Why is she upstairs?"

"She was using the bathroom, Lucia," Lucas told her, keeping his eyes on me.

Alisha stepped past them then went to kiss him, but he moved and mugged her. "I'll holla at you." She smiled softly and nodded.

I tucked my lips in my mouth and stepped to the side, allowing her to leave.

"Go to your room, Lucia," I told her, looking back at my daughter.

She must have heard in my voice that I was pissed because she looked at me then slowly nodded before heading upstairs.

I waited for her to get out of view before I started. "Are you fucking serious, Lucas!" I yelled, unable to keep my feelings under wraps.

"What's the problem, Trinity?"

I stared at him like he was dumb. "You had that bitch here in the house we used to share. In our bed!" my voice cracked.

"We're not together. So what does it matter?"

"What does it matter! We started our family here. We were raising our daughter here and you just have some random bitch in it!"

He stared at me with a blank expression. "What did you come here for?"

I opened my mouth, but no words came out. Lucas was being so insensitive to my feelings right now, and I hated that this was where we were. I know I said some dumb shit to him last night at his warehouse, but I wanted to piss him off and didn't mean it, not entirely at least. I would never allow another man to play daddy to our daughter.

"I saw Trevor today," I told him, shaking the ill feelings out my head. Right now wasn't the time for me to be in my feelings.

"You saw Trevor? Why the fuck was you with that nigga? With my daughter?" He stepped closer to me with a tight face.

"He walked up on us when we were leaving the mall," I quickly told him, seeing how pissed he was.

"What he say?"

I ran down the conversation, and the more I talked the more pissed off Lucas looked.

"You just couldn't keep your damn legs closed, huh!" he finally said.

"Excuse me?"

"That nigga trying to beef over you, Trinity! If you wouldn't have fucked him, then we wouldn't be here."

"Are you blaming me for this? It's clear that Trevor is jealous of you, Lucas! He always has been, I've been told you that!"

"But yet that didn't stop you from sleeping with him!"

"Will you let that go! It's over with. You bringing it up all the time isn't helping anything!"

"No, I won't let that shit go. Because of that he rolled up on you and my fucking daughter! What if he would have tried something? Then what, Trinity! Tell me what you would have done!"

"I don't know Lucas!" I cried.

"You had that nigga thinking he was my daughter's dad and shit. Now he's talking about coming for me because he wants you. All you had to do was stay loyal to me and not open your fucking legs, Trinity. You got in your feelings and now this nigga is a problem!"

"Daddy, stop yelling at mommy!" Lucia came running downstairs past Lucas and hugged my waist. She looked up at me. "Are you okay, mommy?"

I sniffed back my tears and nodded. "I'm fine, Lucia." I ran my hand over her hair.

"Daddy, why are you mad at mommy?" She mugged Lucas.

Lucas licked his lips and his face softened.

"I'm mad at the person you and mommy saw at the mall today."

"Your friend?" Lucas's jaw clenched.

"That's not my friend, Lucia, but yes, him." Lucia looked up at me. "I saw mommy's friend today." She smiled, but my heart dropped.

"Oh, did you?" Lucas crossed his arms.

She nodded. "He was on the phone." My heart stopped.

Lucas stared at me with a hateful glare.

"Lucia, go grab your stuff so we can go," I told her.

"Aww, can we stay? Please, mommy? I want to stay the night with daddy," she begged.

"Lucia."

"You guys are staying, Lucia. Go ahead back upstairs." Lucia happily did what her dad said after making sure I was okay.

"So what nigga you got my daughter talking to?" He stepped closer to me. I had never been scared of Lucas, but the look on his face right now had me terrified.

"I didn't have her talking to anyone. She came into the bathroom when I was on the phone. She heard a male voice and grabbed the phone before I could stop her."

"Who's the nigga?" His eyes narrowed.

"Just a guy I met," I said lowly.

I looked towards the stairs. I could hear Lucas release a deep breath. "You know, every time I try to overlook the shit you did, you do something else to piss me off."

I snapped my head in his direction. "I didn't do shit to you, Lucas! You cheated on me, if you don't remember! Our whole relationship all you did was shit on me, and my stupid ass kept coming back forgiving you!"

"If you feel like that then why did you keep coming back?"

"Because I loved you. I wanted our family! Two things that obviously weren't mutual."

"Here you go with the dramatic shit."

"Dramatic shit? See, that's the problem. You never took our problems seriously. Everything was a joke to you!"

"No, the joke was me believing that I had a real one on my team. All these years, you had me fooled. Trying to call me out on my dirt, but you were holding shit from me. Now you call yourself trying to move on and got my daughter talking to that nigga."

"I-"

"Save that shit, Trinity. Ima handle Trevor. Yall staying here tonight and I don't want to hear no complaints from you." I mugged him.

"I swear I hate you," I mumbled and went to walk past him, but he grabbed me.

"Repeat that shit." I stared at him.

"Leave me alone, Lucas. Don't touch me since you think so lowly of me." I snatched my arm from him then headed upstairs.

Lucas had me deep in my feelings, but I tried to put a brave face on for my daughter when I went into her room. She ended up ditching me to go watch TV with Lucas. I went to the guest room and shut the door. I didn't have shit else to say to Lucas.

CHAPTER 21

BRADY

"Y ALL READY FOR THIS?" I LOOKED AT TARIQ AND LUCAS.

They looked at each other and nodded. Tonight was the night we took out Vicky's baby daddy. He was running around in his feelings since we beat his ass, saying how he was planning on coming for us. A few people I still talked to from our old neighborhood made me aware of the threats, so now it was time to handle it.

I reached behind me and pulled my gun out. None of us took pride in killing anyone. Catching a body was something we tried to avoid. When we were in the streets, it happened like that sometimes. Niggas liked to try you or wanted you to prove your loyalty, but we hadn't had to get our hands dirty since we started the gambling hall.

"Let's get this shit over with," Lucas said, standing up and stretching.

The three of us were dressed in all black. The two of them took their guns out and looked them over just like I had previously done.

"Cool, let's go!" I started towards the door.

Sadly, killing someone lowkey excited me. It wasn't something I was proud of, but I was ready to pull the trigger. I hated for niggas to try me.

Out of everyone, I was quiet and lowkey. Usually, I was laughing and playing peacemaker with everyone until you tried to ruin my peace, then that's when it became a problem.

————

WE ALL SAT in the beat-up car Lucas had gotten ahold of, waiting for the right time to run into the house. Vicky's baby dad Garret had gotten home a little over an hour ago. The only issue was he wasn't alone. He had brought a female home with him.

"Man, I say we go in there shoot his ass then leave," I voiced, getting tired of waiting.

"We not going in there while there's an innocent person in the house with him. I'm sure it won't be too much longer," Tariq commented.

I exhaled loudly and sat back in the seat. My leg began to shake, from me growing even more impatient.

"Nigga, relax. You act like you got somewhere to be." Lucas looked in the mirror at me.

"That's not the point. I didn't come here to watch the nigga's house. I want us to do what we need to do then leave. I'm giving it thirty more minutes than I'm running in there. I'll make sure I don't shoot the girl." Tariq and Lucas made eye contact, but neither of them spoke.

Time continued to pass, and just when I was about to open the door, Garret opened his front door. He said a few words before he kissed her then slapped her ass as she walked away.

"And to think Vicky lost her job because of this nigga," Tariq said.

The girl got in her car and pulled out the driveway. Garret shut the door and the light in his main room went off.

We waited ten minutes after the girl left, making sure she wouldn't double back before grabbing our ski masks and getting out of the car.

"Brady, don't get in here on no extra shit," Tariq called out.

"Yeah, we don't need none of yo little blackout moments."

"Both yall niggas get off my dick." I turned and mugged them.

We walked to the back of the house and stood in front of the back door.

Since I had more weight on me than the other two, I kicked the door open and headed inside.

We checked the house, making sure there was no one else inside before finding Garret's room. He was sitting up in his bed with a blunt in his hand, talking on the phone when we walked in.

"Hang the phone up now!" I yelled. All three of us pointed our guns at him.

His eyes widened then narrowed as he hung the phone up then dropped it.

"What the fuck yall niggas doing here?" he asked, eyeing each of us. I chuckled, you could see that he was nervous, but I had to salute him for trying to hide it.

"I heard you had some words for us pussy," Lucas smirked, snatching his mask off.

"Yall niggas thought yall was going to beat my ass and I let that fly."

"You and yo bitch was stealing from us; what did you expect?" Tariq cocked his gun, causing me and Lucas to follow suit.

"Yall ain't need that extra money. If that stupid bitch wouldn't have outed us, then you wouldn't have known." Tariq lowered his gun and walked towards Garret.

"Nigga, what you doing?" Instead of answering, Tariq got to the bed, raised his gun, and sent it down on Garret's face.

"Watch how you talk about my girl," he said.

He yelled and grabbed his face.

PEW.

Lucas sent a shot out, hitting him in the shoulder. "Disrespect my sister again and I'll make sure you're begging us to kill you," Lucas's voice was low. One thing he didn't play about was Naudia; we all knew that.

I was growing tired of this. There was no point in having a conversation with the nigga anyways. He was now holding his bleeding shoulder, crying out in pain.

I pointed my gun at his head and sent a bullet through it, causing Tariq to jump back. "Nigga you could have warned me." He turned and mugged me.

"I don't get why we were conversing with that nigga for real!" I turned and left out of the room with the two of them behind me.

We walked out the back door the same way we came in and got in the car. We all were quiet for a minute.

"That shit went smooth. Hopefully, no one else tries us," Tariq commented.

I noticed Lucas gripped the steering wheel. "I'm killing Trevor," he suddenly said.

"For that Trinity shit?"

Lucas's face grew more tense. "Nah, he approached her, threatening me while my daughter was with her. When I find that nigga, I'm putting one between his eyes."

My eyes widened. "Oh yeah, that nigga needs to be dealt with."

"I knew that nigga was dirty but damn." Tariq shook his head.

We were all quiet in our thoughts. If I ever found out Renee fucked one of my niggas, I wasn't sure how I would react. I knew that it was fucking with Lucas, especially since we grew up with that nigga, used to eat with that nigga. Yet, I knew Trinity still loved Lucas.

Trevor always had some envy in him towards Lucas. Anyone with eyes could see it. It didn't make sense at first. Not until the shit with Trinity came out. Now the nigga was about to lose his life for some pussy that didn't even belong to him.

———

"WHAT'S ALL THIS?" Renee asked, smiling when she walked into my house.

I handed her the bags in my hands and kissed her cheek.

"I told you we were going to celebrate your grades. It just had to get pushed back a few days."

She smiled and I waved for her to follow me. We walked to my living room and I sat down while she opened her gifts.

The first bag was a pair of pink, orange, and white *VaporMaxs*. She looked at me and I nodded, encouraging her to continue looking.

Reaching back into the bag, she pulled out the *Cartier* box and opened it. "Baby!" she shrieked.

In the box was the rose gold bracelet from their Love collection I had seen her looking at a few weeks ago, along with some earrings.

She dropped the stuff and ran over to me, jumping in my lap. "I love it, thank you, baby!" She kissed me passionately and starting grinding against me.

"We have reservations we're going to miss if you don't chill out," I warned her feeling my dick growing in my jeans.

"Let's miss them." Lust dripped from her voice.

I grabbed her ass, squeezing it. "Your ass done got juicier." I shook my hand, making her ass shake.

She giggled and I stood up. Her legs went around my waist and we continued to kiss as I walked to my room.

"I swear I don't know what you did, but I can't get enough of you," I told her once I was in her.

Her face was twisting in some sexy ass sex faces. Her moans were low, and she was throwing her body against mine. I had her legs in the crook of my arms as I moved in and out of her.

"Damn Renee, I know it's been a few days but let up," I groaned, feeling her pussy gripping my dick tightly.

"You feel so good, Brady!" Her eyes opened and she made eye contact with me before her eyes rolled to the back of her head. It seemed like her pussy grew ten times wetter as she came. I looked down with my eyebrow raised.

Biting down on my bottom lip, I let her legs go and pulled out. "I'm trying to see this ass from the back." I massaged her clit and looked down at her.

She stared at me with low eyes before nodding and flipping over. She put an arch in her back, and I licked my lips. Her ass really had grown, and her pussy was looking juicy as fuck from behind.

I bent down and ran my tongue over her pussy and she jumped. I grabbed her hips and started eating her pussy from behind.

"Brady!" she cried but started throwing her ass back to fuck my face.

I kept kissing and sucking on her pussy until I felt she was about to cum again and then plunged my dick back into her.

"Renee, what the fuck is going on with yo pussy right now?" I mumbled.

I spread her ass so I could have more access to go deeper. Renee attempted to run, but I held her hips.

"Wait, Brady!" She reached behind her to try and push on my stomach, but I smacked her hand away.

"Stop fucking playing with me!" I growled, moving faster in and out of her.

Her moans grew louder and I could feel myself about to cum.

I reached forward and grabbed the back of Renee's neck, slightly squeezing it. "Renee, I want you to cum with me, baby. Make that pussy leak for me," I said, pushing deep in her.

"Pull out, Brady!" she begged but started throwing her ass back faster.

My eyebrows furrowed together as I thought her words over. I looked down at my bare dick moving in and out of her when my eyes widened.

"Brady! What are you doing?" Renee turned around yelling when I snatched out of her. "I was close," she whined.

I ignored her and hurried to my phone on my dresser. My eyebrows stayed knitted together as I pulled up my calendar.

"Why aren't you on your period right now?" I asked her, looking up from my phone.

She gave me a confused look. "You really stopped having sex to ask me that?"

I licked my lips and gave her a once over. "You're supposed to be on your period right now. Why aren't you?"

"How do you know that?"

"Renee, is your period supposed to be on right now or not?" She rolled her eyes then went to her shorts on the ground and grabbed her phone up. After clicking her phone a few times, her eyes raised to meet mine. By now my dick had gone down.

"It doesn't mean anything," her voice was low.

I smirked.

"Your period is always on time, Renee."

"Brady, how the hell do you know so much about my period?"

"I need to know when my pussy is out of commission, so I keep track," I shrugged.

Her mouth dropped. "You're crazy."

"And I think you're pregnant." Her eyes darted away from mine and she stared at her phone again.

"It's only a few days late. I been worried about my grades and stuff, I probably just got thrown off."

I walked up on her. "You're gaining weight." I pinched her swollen nipple, taking in the fact that they had grown too.

"Your pussy was snugger too, and I couldn't even hit that shit from the back like I normally do." She licked her lips and ran her fingers through her hair.

"That doesn't mean anything."

I bent down so that I was eye level with her stomach and touched it. "What, you don't want to have my baby?"

She flinched and stared down at me. Tears filled her eyes. "Damn, it's that bad." I removed my hand, feeling myself getting pissed off.

"You know what happened to me the last time I was pregnant," she said.

I stood up, sat on the bed, and pulled her on my lap. "That happened because you were fucking with a bitch ass nigga. I would never allow anything to happen to you or my baby."

She stared at me worried and sighed. "Let's just see if my period comes. If it's not here by next week, I'll take a test." I wasn't happy with her answer, but I didn't fight her on it.

I pulled her face to mine and kissed her. Renee could try to fight it all she wanted, but I was sure she was pregnant with my baby.

CHAPTER 22

TARIQ

I yawned and walked into my bedroom. A nigga couldn't wait to slide in my bed and sleep. I felt like I had been on go for the last few days and I needed sleep.

I attempted to be quiet so that I wouldn't wake Naudia, but to my surprise, she was woke when I walked into my room.

"What's up, baby? What you doing up?" She jumped and stared at me.

"You alright?" I asked concerned, making my way to the bed.

I crawled up to her and touched her leg. She jerked it out of my reach.

"Naudia, what's wrong?" I was taken aback when I looked at her and noticed she looked terrified.

"I saw him," she finally said.

I looked around my room. "Saw who, baby?" Swallowing hard, she finally made eye contact with me.

"Danny. When I was asleep, he was above me smiling at me, trying to touch me." I sighed heavily and chewed on my bottom lip.

"Baby, that nigga isn't anywhere around here."

"But he's still out there. What if he catches me out and tries to drug me again? Or worse, what if he-"

"He won't," I cut her off before she could even finish her sentence. I didn't even want to think of that nigga touching her.

"I fucked up by letting him get away with what he did this long. You got my word I'm going to handle him soon."

She stared at me with unsure eyes. "Promise?" her voice was almost kid-like.

I nodded. "How long you been feeling like this?" I asked her.

Naudia shrugged. "Since it happened. At first, I was able to push it to the back of my head, but the nightmares are becoming more frequent. Then I woke up and I was alone, and I just got freaked out."

My jaw clenched. "Why didn't you tell me this?"

Once again, she shrugged. "I didn't want to burden you. I thought I would be fine if I didn't talk about it."

"Baby if something is bothering you, you should feel comfortable enough to talk to me because I'm your man, ain't I?"

She shyly smiled and nodded her head.

I moved up on the bed then grabbed her chin. "As your man, I'm here to help you through whatever problems you have. We're a team, baby." I pulled her face down to kiss her.

Her smile grew against my mouth. "Come get in the shower with me." I sat up.

Naudia climbed out of bed and followed me to the bathroom.

As soon as we stepped in the shower, I was on Naudia. I pushed her to the shower wall as the water beat down on us. Her chest pressed against the wall while I pushed my dick in her. I grabbed her by her now wet hair and yanked her head back.

"I miss your braids, but I love gripping this shit," I moaned, moving in and out of her.

I kissed on the side of her neck, sucking on it roughly.

Naudia, never the one to be lazy during sex, started throwing her hips back against mine and matched my stroke.

I drilled her from behind. She turned her head to look at me. We made eye contact and our lips connected. Naudia pulled on my tongue and moaned softly in my mouth.

"Your pussy feels so good, Naudia. Your little young ass got me strung out and shit," I groaned, pumping in and out of her faster.

"Riq!" she cried, squeezing her mouth shut.

I pulled back and turned her around, picking her up. I fucked her from below while she bounced up and down on my pole. Her arms circled my neck.

"Tariq," she moaned softly.

I stared at her. "What's up, baby?"

"Don't ever leave me, Tariq. Don't ever take this dick from me." I smirked and pressed her back against the wall.

I slowed down my movements making sure to push deep inside her.

"You're mine Naudia. I'm not going anywhere, and neither are you. Do you hear me?" She gripped my shoulders and started breathing heavily.

"Do you hear me, baby?" I moved closer to her, allowing my lips to brush against hers.

Naudia stared at me and slowly nodded her head. "I hear you baby. I'm not going anywhere."

We kissed again, and before long, both of us were cumming.

Naudia and I finished up in the shower then got in bed. She was laying on my chest while I held her tightly.

"Naudia, I'm not going to allow anyone else to hurt you. I'm going to handle that Danny nigga and we're going to move on from it, okay?"

She looked up at me. "Okay." Leaning down, I kissed her forehead and held her tighter.

Seeing how scared Naudia was because of some pussy nigga didn't sit right with me and made me feel like as her man, I was failing her. I should have been putting more effort into finding that nigga and making sure she felt safe after all that happened to her.

Since she was putting on as if she was fine, I didn't think about it, but now I felt like I was neglecting her.

"Tariq," Naudia whispered, breaking me from my thoughts.

"What's up, baby?"

She was quiet for a second. "I don't want to move out. I know it's too soon for us to be living together, but we've known each other our whole lives, and I don't want to feel like I forced myself into your life, but I just, I feel safe with you."

I ran my hand through her damp hair as I felt her chest rising and falling against mine.

"I don't have an issue with you being here," I finally told her.

She looked up at me. "You sure? I don't want to rush things."

"Naudia, I want you here and I don't mind you being here. You can stay as long as you want. I don't have any problem with that." She smiled softly at me and lowered her head.

The tired feeling I felt when I first got home had started to overcome me again.

———

I LOOKED DOWN at my phone, making sure I had the right address before climbing out of the car.

The street was pretty much abandoned. When I got to the door, I turned my phone off, pulled my hat low on my face, and knocked on the door.

"Who is it?" Instead of answering, I knocked again.

"I said who is it?" The door was snatched open.

Danny stood in front of me with a mug on his face. "Who are you?" he questioned.

"You Danny?"

"Yeah, why?" I smirked and rushed him, causing him to stumble back.

I kicked the door shut and sent my fist crashing into his face. He went crashing on the ground and I didn't let up.

"You like drugging women, right?" I asked, hitting him again.

He groaned out in pain as I continued hitting him. I didn't let up until I grew tired.

Standing over him, I stared down at him with angry eyes. He was curled up crying out, coughing blood out.

"I, I'm sorry," he mumbled, spitting blood out his mouth.

"Shut up!" I kicked him in the stomach with my boot. He grunted and grabbed his stomach.

I wasn't a murderer, but I knew that Naudia wouldn't feel comfortable if this nigga was still running around. Reaching in my hood pocket, I grabbed my gun, making sure the silencer was tight on it.

"Wait, please-" Before he could finish, I cocked the gun and sent a bullet through his head silencing him.

I heard noise coming from the back of the house and what sounded like a garage closing.

I began to panic. Quickly turning around, I rushed out the door. Since I had gloves on, I wasn't worried about fingerprints. I rushed to the same car we used to kill Garret and hurried down the street.

Sighing once I was a safe distance from the house, I grabbed my phone and turned it on. Ignoring the notifications coming in, I called Naudia.

"Hey you!" she answered, sounding like she was smiling.

"Where you at?" I was on the way to the warehouse to switch cars.

"At Renee's."

"Cool, stay there. I'm on my way."

I hung the phone up, not worrying about her replying, and kept driving.

After switching cars and making sure the dump car was hidden in the back. I quickly changed my clothes before making my way to Renee's house. Once I was close, I texted Naudia telling her to come outside.

I got out of the car and had to adjust myself. Naudia was in a sundress that looked good as hell on her.

"Hey, what's wrong?" She stared at me worried.

I pulled her into me and hugged her tightly.

"You know how I said I was going to handle that situation for you?" I looked down at her.

It looked like she was in deep thought before it finally came to her and she nodded.

"It's handled. You don't ever have to worry about that nigga again." She stared at me in amazement.

"You're serious?" I grinned.

"Yeah, girl. I told you I was going to handle it, right?"

Naudia threw her arms around my neck and hugged me tightly. Soon I felt a wet spot on my shirt.

"Thank you," she cried into my chest.

I rubbed her back and kissed the top of her head.

"Stop crying, man. I told you I would handle it." She looked up at me and smiled widely.

"You're amazing! I don't deserve you." She hugged me tightly again.

I couldn't cap and say hearing her admit that didn't make a nigga feel good.

"Aye, look at me," I commanded.

First sniffing tears back, Naudia looked at me with that innocent look on her face. "Don't say that. You have your flaws but we all do." She leaned up and kissed me.

"How much longer you gone be here?"

"I can leave now."

I nodded.

"Let's go grab something to eat then head home."

"Okay!" She let me go then headed back towards the house while I turned and headed for my car.

While I was waiting on her, I texted my cousin.

Good Look.

I ended up getting the nigga Danny's number out of Naudia's phone and sending it to my cousin to track. He was able to get his address for me easily.

I watched Naudia walk out of the house then to my passenger side.

"You leaving your car?"

"Renee picked me up."

I nodded and threw my car in drive.

On the way to the restaurant, Naudia looked over at me.

"Thank you, Tariq."

I grabbed her hand and squeezed it.

Naudia didn't have to keep thanking me because I cared about her. I was starting to care more and more for her as the days went on. If anyone threatened to bring harm to her, I had no problem handling it for her.

CHAPTER 23

RENEE

Ever since Brady made a comment about me possibly being pregnant, I'd been freaking out. When I went back and checked, I saw I was a month late, but I chalked it up to stressing about school and finals. Plus, I was going through a lot when my due date from my first pregnancy came around.

I looked myself over in the mirror, turning around to stare at my backside, and realized that I had gained some weight. Hell, I chalked that shit up to happy weight. They say when you're getting good dick and you're happy, it happens. I haven't been sick or anything like I was with my first pregnancy.

I honestly thought Brady was just talking. It still amazed me that his ass tracked my periods. I didn't think he paid that much attention to me.

"So you ready?" I looked up and made eye contact with Brady.

He came by this morning so we could get the pregnancy test. I thought he would let it go, but he for real gave me a week, and with me still not having a period, he was convinced I was pregnant.

"Brady, I'm telling you I'm not pregnant. I've been pregnant before and I don't have any of the signs."

"Besides your weight gain and missing period, right?" He crossed his arms and tilted his head to the side.

I turned to face him. "I feel like you're telling me I'm getting fat."

His eyes roamed my body. "I'm telling you that you didn't have that much weight on you a few months ago. Look at your chest, Renee. You're damn near spilling out your bra."

I looked back at the mirror and had to admit he was right. I was normally a thirty-four-C and my bras always fit perfectly.

"They probably shrunk," I tried to convince myself.

Brady walked up to me and wrapped his arms around me from behind. Moving my ponytail out the way, he kissed the back of my neck a few times.

"Renee, I know you went through some shit with your first pregnancy, but baby, you can't keep denying something is up with your body." He gripped me tighter and his hands gravitated to my stomach.

"You have to accept it." I closed my eyes and rested my hands over his.

"I'm just scared." He kissed my neck again and rested his lips on it for a few seconds.

"I would never put you in a position for something like what happened to you to occur again. That's on my life. You and our baby will be good." I slowly opened my eyes and saw he was staring at me.

Inhaling a deep breath, I released it and nodded. "Okay, let's go get a test," I told him.

Brady smiled.

"Have faith in your man, alright?"

I forced a smile on my face and nodded. "I do." That I did,

Brady was so real with his shit I know he would never hurt me purposely.

———

I WAS in line waiting to pay for the pregnancy test I had just picked up. My stomach was in knots the closer I got to the counter. Honestly, I don't even know why I was nervous. If I was pregnant, it wouldn't be horrible, *right?*

Brady was a great guy. He was everything I could ask for when it came to a man. No matter what his day looked like, he always reached out to me if he didn't hear from me. Considering we used to go days without talking, that was a dramatic change for us. We were now at a place in our relationship where we hardly slept away from one another, and we'd even exchanged house keys. Since he usually got in late, he would come to my house. It got to the point where it felt weird if he wasn't next to me at night.

The more I thought about me and Brady's relationship, the more I realized I had slowly fallen in love with him, which scared me. Brady and I were just sex at first, and out of nowhere, everything changed. I wasn't sure how he felt about everything. It felt like he loved me, but I had never seen Brady serious with anyone, so it was hard to tell. He was a playboy before we got together. There were times I still wondered if he was out sleeping around.

I looked up and realized I was next in line. I took a deep breath and walked up to the counter and sat the test down.

After paying for the test, I snatched the bag off the counter and headed out the doors. My nerves were starting to grow now.

"Renee!" That voice. *Why couldn't he just take the hint?*

"Leave me alone," I called over my shoulder.

"Renee, hold on, man!" My arms were grabbed, and Matt turned me around.

"Don't touch me!" I jerked my arm out of his grasp.

He tossed his hands up. "I just want to talk to you. Damn, is that so bad?" I stared at Matt like he had lost his mind. He had this desperate look on his face like he wasn't the one to cause me so much pain.

"What do we have to talk about, Matt? All our reasons to talk died when I lost my child."

He sighed and ran a hand over his head. Matt licked his pink lips and looked around the parking lot.

"I know that you hold a lot of hate for me because of that. It's something I'll regret for the rest of my life but-," he paused when he looked down. His eyes squinted and his eyebrows bunched together.

"Wow, you're pregnant?" I looked down at the bag in my hand. The store used clear bags, showcasing the test.

"That's none of your business. Now please, next time you see me, don't speak!" I tried to leave, but he grabbed my arm again.

"Renee!"

When I was about to snatch away from him again, a fist crashed into his face, causing me to yell. I stumbled back from me being suddenly let go.

"I guess you didn't learn last time!" Brady yelled, hitting him again.

"Brady!" I yelled, trying to get him to stop.

Instead of listening, he kept hitting Matt. Matt attempted to fight back, but Brady was in rare form. My eyes widened as I watched Matt fall to the ground. Brady got over him, still hitting him and ignoring my yells.

I ran over and grabbed his arm. He yanked away from me and I stumbled back some. Brady looked over his shoulder. The look on his face sent a chill through my body.

"Baby, let's go," I said softly. He was breathing hard, his nose flared, and he was in mid-punch.

"Brady, baby, please come on," I said, stepping closer. My heart was about to beat out of my chest.

Thankfully, the parking lot was empty, so there was no attention on us, but still, I wanted to go.

"If you come near my girl again, no one will be able to stop me," he told Matt and stood up.

I swallowed hard and looked at Matt. He was on the ground, curled up and groaning in pain. I lowkey felt sorry for him. Brady had turned into someone else. The look on his face didn't even look like he knew what was going on when I grabbed him.

I followed behind Brady and we got in the car. Neither of us spoke as he drove. He went to grab my hand, but I moved it away. Out the corner of my eye, I could see him glare at me, but I ignored it.

Soon as we got into my house, I jumped out of the car, hurried to my door, unlocked it, and rushed to the bathroom. Part of the reason was that my bladder was about to explode. The other, I needed a second away from Brady.

I knew he had his moments where he blacked out. I'd heard about it, but I never actually seen it.

After peeing on the stick and washing my hands, I sat the test on my sink and walked into my bedroom.

Brady was sitting on the bed with his head down in his phone. He slowly looked up at me while I stood in place. Right now, he looked like my Brady.

"So?" he asked.

"It says we wait three minutes," I said quietly.

Brady tossed his phone on my bed and stepped closer to me. My body stiffened. When he moved to grab me, I flinched. He took a step back and stared at me curiously. His eyebrow raised.

"You for real?" he asked.

"What was that?" I countered.

"That nigga shouldn't have touched you."

"You're right, he shouldn't have, but what you did was overkill, wasn't it?"

"Renee, you know I don't play about people I love. He shouldn't have grabbed you. Shit, he shouldn't even have been in your damn face."

I heard what he was saying, but I was stuck on one thing. "So you love me?" I asked, staring into his eyes.

He licked his lips and smirked. Stepping closer to me, he went to grab me again. This time I didn't flinch, but my body was still slightly tensed.

"I do." He bent down and pecked my lips. "Sometimes when I get mad, I get carried away. I didn't like seeing him grab you. My mind went blank at that moment. I didn't mean to scare you."

"When you looked at me, you looked like you were going to hit me next. I wasn't sure what to do," I confessed.

Brady's face balled up. He pulled his bottom lip between his teeth and grabbed my hips.

"I will never put my hands on you or any other woman. If I get like that, don't touch me though, I don't be thinking right. I don't want you to be scared of me though. I don't like you flinching and shit when I come close to you."

I stared into his eyes. My body finally relaxed. I nodded and wrapped my arms around his neck. Stretching my neck, I kissed him.

"I love you too," I said against his lips.

We stood there kissing for a minute until he pulled away.

"Don't be trying to distract me." He grabbed my hand and pulled me towards the bathroom, causing me to laugh.

"Well?" I asked when he looked at the test.

"Here." He handed it to me.

I slowly reached for the test and looked down at it. I grew nauseated when I saw the plus sign.

"Oh shit," I mumbled.

I willed the tears not to cloud my eyes. I looked up at Brady, who had a huge smile on his face.

"We're having a baby," I said, more so to myself.

"We're having a baby!" He snatched me up, catching me off guard.

Brady sat me on the sink and forced himself between my legs.

"We got this. You and our baby will be fine," he assured me. The smile on his face never went away.

"Do you trust me?" he asked me.

"I do."

"Then know I got you. Both of you."

I licked my lips. "Okay."

Brady ended up not going to the gambling hall that night. Instead, he stayed the night with me. He was excited about this baby, whereas I was still on the fence.

CHAPTER 24

NAUDIA

"WHY YOU LOOK SO SAD?" TRINITY ASKED ME.

I stared at her then looked back down at my phone, replying to the message Nick just sent me before I answered her.

"I have no idea what to do with myself."

She looked confused. "Naudia, what the hell are you talking about?" she snickered.

"I mean, just what I said. Since I'm not in school anymore and I don't work, I have no idea what I want to do with my life," I sighed and looked at my phone.

Rolling my eyes, I tossed it to the side. "Well, what did you do before when you weren't in school."

"Party and have sex." Trinity's mouth dropped before she shook her head.

"I'm being for real, Naudia."

"Hell, me too! I never took college seriously. I just wanted my brother off my back. I told him I would find something to do with my life since I didn't want to do school anymore, and I have yet to figure it out."

"Well, what do you like doing?" I thought about her question. Hell, I didn't even know what I liked to do. It used to be partying, drinking, and having sex. I wasn't really a shopping person, even though I could fuck up some commas when I wanted to.

"Gambling."

She nodded. "So why not try and work at the gambling hall?"

I started laughing until I saw Trinity was serious. "Trinity, come on, you know my brother is not going for that."

"Girl, fuck your brother," she paused and waved me off. "Your man owns part of it too, right? Talk to Tariq," she shrugged.

"I doubt he'll let me either."

"Naudia, you're one of the best blackjack players I've ever seen. It's not like you'll be in there drinking. You'll be working, and hell, if they say no, ask to work the bar. You know your way around the bar."

The thought did sound good, but I wasn't sure if Lucas or Tariq would let me work at the gambling hall. Lucas already didn't like me there, and Tariq would be on my ass all night. Still, it wouldn't hurt to ask.

"You're right. I'll talk to the two of them and see what they say."

"Good!" Trinity picked her phone up. A wide grin appeared on her face while she texted back whoever had just texted her.

I took a moment to text Nick back. I was trying to figure out when he was going to be home. Tariq wasn't happy that I hadn't cut him off yet. The other day we got into an argument about it. I told him Nick was just a friend, but he wasn't for it being that Nick and I had slept together.

"Who got you over there smiling?" I asked Trinity.

She looked up from her phone blushing. "Girl and you blushing. Who is it?"

Trinity giggled. "His name is Myles."

"Myles, huh? Where did you meet him?"

"At the sandwich shop up the street from where I work at."

I smiled. "From the way you're smiling, I can tell you like him."

She slowly nodded her head. "We went out for drinks and things went good. The conversation flowed and he was such a gentleman."

I stared at Trinity, having mixed feelings about this. I'm happy she was moving on. I kept telling my brother that his chances with her would eventually run out, especially with him being in his feelings right now. On the other hand, Trinity deserved to be happy with someone that treated her right. If my brother wasn't going to get it together, then she deserved to move on.

"I can tell by the look on your face you don't like this," Trinity laughed.

I shook my head. "It's not that I don't like it. I'm happy that you're moving on and not letting Lucas keep you in your feelings. I just wish you two would work it out. I love you two together, yall been together half my life."

Trinity shifted some in her seat. "I know it was weird at first. Hell, I haven't been out with anyone besides your brother in ten years. The thought of having to get to know someone new is scary as hell. Sadly, a small part of me wants to fix things with your brother. I still love him, but I can't sit around and wait for him."

I nodded. "I agree. You deserve to be happy. If being with someone else makes you happy, then so be it. If he has a sister though tell her the spot is filled and not up for grabs."

"Girl, it's not even that deep," she stopped and laughed. "We went out once. Outside of texting and FaceTiming, we haven't been able to meet up."

"Why?"

"Our schedules just clash. With Lucia, I can't just go out whenever he's free, and then he works. It's just hard."

"Makes sense. Does my brother know?" Trinity frowned.

"Yeah, he does."

I grinned. "How did that go?"

"How do you think it went. He was pissed. It didn't help that Lucia was the one that told him." She poked her lips out.

My eyes widened. "Wait she met him?"

"Girl, no. Lucas would kill me if I had another man around her. He was on FaceTime and she walked in grabbing my phone," Trinity explained.

My phone went off and it was Nick telling me he was about to be home.

I stood up. "I have to go handle something. I'm still rooting for you and my brother, but I won't hate on you for attempting to move on."

"Well, thank you," Trinity laughed.

I turned and headed for the door, praying this would go smooth.

———

"DAMN GIRL, you're a hard person to track down." Nick grabbed me and pulled me into him.

He tried to kiss me, but I moved my head. "Nick, we need to talk," I told him.

He started kissing down my face to my neck. His hands went to the jeans I had on.

"Nick!" I called out, grabbing his hand.

"What's up, baby?" He kissed on my neck again.

I took a deep breath and tried not to react to him. "I didn't come here for this." I pushed him away.

"What's up, Naudia? I haven't seen you in a while, and that's not even like us." He started undressing me with his eyes.

"We can't do this anymore," I finally told him.

"Do what?"

I pointed between the two of us. "This whatever it was we were doing."

"Man, Naudia, quit playing with me." He took a step towards me, but I stepped back from him.

"I'm not playing, Nick. I'm with someone now."

'So what does that mean?"

"What the hell do you think it means? Me and you can't fuck anymore. He doesn't like that you hit my phone up either, so you need to stop."

"Damn, for real? Wed been rocking for three years. I mentioned us being together and you blew me off each time. Now all of a sudden you're in a relationship?"

I sighed. "I liked the arrangement we had, but I don't know, things changed."

"So you liked being a hoe up until now?" I frowned.

"Nigga what?"

"I mean, come on, Naudia. Do you know how many niggas used to talk about sleeping with you? I used to ignore that shit because we vibed well together, but don't act like you ain't know your name was out there."

"I don't give a fuck what niggas said they slept with me; if you didn't hear it from me, then you shouldn't believe it." Nick chuckled and shook his head.

"Naudia, me and you both know what kind of girl you are. Niggas knew that so they used that to their advantage."

I swallowed hard. "So why did you keep trying to make shit official with me?"

"Shit, my ass fell for you before I realized how much you were out here. Not to mention you had some good pussy. Why would I want a lot of niggas feeling that?" He shrugged.

I was speechless. "Fuck you, Nick. You act like you weren't out here."

"I was but I'm a nigga. You're a female, you opening your legs to whoever isn't cool."

Nick's words cut me deep. I used to hear shit from my brother, and females used to talk shit to me, but I never really thought niggas were out here talking shit about me.

"Well, I guess it's a good thing I have a nigga now."

"Yeah, I guess," he shrugged.

Instead of saying anything else to him, I turned to leave.

"Aye, if you get tired of fucking the same nigga my door is always open," Nick called out behind me.

I closed my eyes and opened his door and walked out the door.

———

"NAUDIA, why the hell are you sitting in here with the lights off?" Tariq walked into the living room.

Instead of answering him, I continued to stare at the wall in front of me.

Tariq took a seat next to me. "Naudi, baby, what's wrong? Why are you crying?" He wiped the tears running down my face.

"Are people out there talking about me?" I asked him.

"Talking about you?"

I turned my head to look at him. "Yes, Tariq, talking about me."

His silence spoke volumes to me. I closed my eyes and clenched my fist together. "Naudia, where is this coming from?"

"I stopped sleeping around, I chilled out, I haven't slept with anyone's boyfriend, I haven't been out here being careless."

"I know that shit; why are you telling me that?"

His eyes squinted. Tariq grabbed my chin and tilted my head.

"Who the fuck was sucking on your neck?" My eyes grew. I

slapped my hand on my neck and wiped it as if whatever was there would come off.

"I didn't do anything!" I told him.

He stood up and hovered me. "So how the fuck did a hickey get on your neck Naudia? I didn't put that shit there!"

I swallowed hard. More tears started running down my face.

"I'm not falling for that crying shit, Naudia. You been messing around on me?"

"No, Tariq!"

"So where the fuck did it come from?"

"I don't know," I cried.

I could see his jaw clench. "That's yo final answer?"

I knew I didn't do anything, but the way Tariq was staring at me right now had me feeling like I did. I knew I needed to hurry up and explain myself before this got worse. I didn't even know Nick did this shit. I was so focused on what he said to me that I didn't think about when he was kissing on me.

"I'm not doing this shit with you, man." He shook his head and stood up.

My chest clenched. I hurriedly jumped up, rushing to him.

"Tariq, I didn't do anything," I cried.

"So who the fuck was sucking on your neck Naudia!" He turned and yelled, causing me to jump.

"I, I went to see Nick today. When I first got there, he was all on me. I pushed him off though and told him we couldn't see each other anymore."

Tariq glared at me. "You expect me to believe that shit?"

"It's the truth!"

"He must have been kissing on you for a while for you to have that shit on you, Naudia. Get the fuck out of here with that stupid shit. You fucked that nigga?"

My mouth dropped. "NO! I just told you what happened."

Tariq released a pissed off chuckle and grabbed on his beard.

"I knew this shit was going to happen. I should have went with my fucking gut."

I cocked my head back and wiped my eyes. "What's that supposed to mean?"

"It means you're still on the same fucking bullshit. I told you I wasn't dealing with that bullshit, Naudia. I'm cool on this shit!" He turned and headed in the direction of his door.

"Tariq!" I yelled out to him.

Tariq didn't stop though, he ignored me and kept walking.

"Tariq, I didn't do anything!" I cried.

I stood there in shock that he just had walked away from me. I couldn't believe he didn't believe me. Given I knew my track record, but I would never do that to him.

I stood in the same spot waiting for him to walk back through the door, but he never came.

Sucking my tears up, I headed for the stairs.

I wasn't in the business of staying with a nigga who didn't want me. Secretly I was waiting for this moment to happen. I knew nothing good last forever.

CHAPTER 25

TARIQ

I HAD TO GET AWAY FROM NAUDIA BEFORE I SAID SOME SHIT I couldn't take back. Just thinking of her being with someone else had me ready to put a bullet in someone.

The bad part is I wanted to believe her. The way she cried to me had me wanting to believe she didn't fuck anyone, but the fact that her past was sketchy had me second-guessing her. I wanted to believe that Naudia easily changed, but there were still parts of me that had doubts.

I gripped the steering wheel thinking of the hickey of her neck, then bit down on my bottom lip thinking of someone else between her legs.

My phone vibrated. I opened it and saw it was Naudia calling in. I ignored the call and the call after that. I ain't have shit to say with her.

The size of the hickey was decent. If she would have just pushed the nigga off like she said, then he wouldn't have been able to make that shit. Something more had to happen.

I pulled up back at the gambling hall and cut my car off.

I tried to calm down before I walked in here.

"I thought you weren't coming until later?" Lucas asked when I walked in.

"Yeah, well change of plans." I walked over to the bar to make myself a shot.

"Damn nigga, what's wrong with you?"

My phone went off. I pulled it out and looked at the screen. Seeing it was Chyna, I ignored the call. I didn't want to talk to her ass either.

"Your damn sister." I tossed the shot back then poured another.

Lucas walked over to the bar and took a seat. "She started giving yo ass a run for yo money, huh?" Lucas started laughing, but when he saw I wasn't in a laughing mood, he stopped.

"What she do?"

Lucas was my nigga, but I didn't feel comfortable discussing my relationship with his sister with him.

"Same shit she always does," I took another shot to the head before closing the bottle.

"She fucking around?"

"Shit, she said she isn't, but I don't believe that shit."

My phone vibrated. I looked and saw once again it was Chyna. This time I answered. "I'm not in the mood right now. Stop calling me," I told her and hung up before she could speak. I put my phone on DND and stuck it in my pocket.

"That better not have been my sister you just talked to like that," Lucas frowned.

"Nah," was all I told him.

"What up niggas!" Brady walked in cheesing.

"Nigga you been in a good ass mood lately. What's up?" Lucas asked him.

Brady walked over and sat down next to him. "I don't know if she wants people to know yet but fuck it, it's mine too. Renee is pregnant."

"Aye, that's what's up, man. Congrats!" Lucas slapped hands with him.

"Yeah nigga, congrats."

"Appreciate it. That shit done had me smiling since I found out. Yall know how shitty my dad was. I can't wait to be the complete opposite of that nigga."

"I feel that shit. I love being a father. Even if I did drop the ball a few times, I wouldn't trade this shit."

I tuned them out. Right now I wasn't trying to talk about kids and shit.

"What's wrong with this nigga? Why he look like he ready to fight?" Brady asked, nodding towards me.

"Shit, hell if I know. Something happened with him and my sister."

"Yall having issues already?"

I glared at him. "Naudia just knows how to piss a nigga off."

"She must have did some real shit to have you in yo feelings like a bitch," Brady laughed, and Lucas joined in.

I chuckled.

He was right. I have never been this pissed off when it came to a female. The thought of Naudia being with someone else had me wanting to wring her damn neck. I was planning on us going out to eat or something before I came in tonight too. All that went out the window when I saw that damn hickey though.

"I ain't even trying to talk about that shit.." I waved them both off.

"Well, let's talk about the pills. I know you haven't gotten any the past few weeks. What the fuck is up with that? I thought we were just slowing down?"

"That nigga Tech been on some bullshit. Took some vacation or some shit. He just hit me up though saying he'll be back in two weeks and I can get an order."

Lucas nodded. "Good, the hall is doing better than I expected, but that extra money wasn't hurting anything."

"Yeah, the hall has been increasing like a muthafucka. We need to invest this money to clean it."

Brady looked down at his phone. "This my moms. I'll be right back." He stepped off to the side.

"I have been thinking about that. Especially since we're being investigated. I just don't know what the hell we would invest in."

I was about to answer when Brady went flying past us out the door.

"Brady!" We both called out rushing after him.

By the time we got outside he was in his car skirting off.

"What the hell was that about?"

"Shit, yo guess is as good as mine." I shrugged.

"Let's go in here and start setting up. I'm sure that nigga will call us soon and let us know what's up." Lucas headed back into the warehouse.

I took my phone out of my pocket to see if Naudia had tried to contact me again. I grew even more pissed seeing she hadn't, but Chyna had.

This had me second-guessing if I made the right choice choosing Naudia over Chyna. With Chyna, I didn't have to worry about her messing around on me. She was a little clingy sometimes and needed to learn to control her attitude, but she was loyal no matter what bullshit I put her through.

I shook my head.

Even if I would have stayed with Chyna, I knew it wouldn't have worked out in the long run. The feelings had I had for Naudia were stronger, how I'm feeling right now proved it.

I opened the message from Chyna, and I had to read that shit twice.

I just wanted to let you know I was pregnant but I'm getting an abortion.

CHAPTER 26

BRADY

I RUSHED OUT OF THE WAREHOUSE TO MY CAR, NOT BOTHERING TO tell Lucas or Tariq what was up. I needed to get to my mom's house.

She called me hysterical, telling me she received a call that my dad had been approved for parole and would be out soon.

My eyes narrowed as I sped down the road. I couldn't believe they were letting that nigga out after he tried to kill my mom. She was terrified of that nigga. It took her years to finally stop flinching when someone approached her.

She hasn't dated that I know of since the incident with my dad. He had broken her, changed her. No matter how much I tried to get her to get back to the old her, she just couldn't. All the years of abuse she took from my dad had messed her up.

I hated she waited so long to leave him. To this day I couldn't understand what made her stay as long as she did. For as long as I could remember my dad used to beat my mom, and once I got older, he started on me.

Secretly I resented my mom for a long time for dealing with my dad as long as she did. I felt like she was weak for never leaving him but then I realized my dad had some type of hold on her. He had broken my mom so bad that she felt like she couldn't live without him,

The day I got to her house and saw her inches away from dying was embedded in my head to this day. The look on my dad's face showed that he would have really killed her if he wasn't stopped. Every day I wish I could go back to that day and kill that nigga.

He was a shitty dad my whole life. Always bitching and yelling over stupid shit. When I got old enough to fight back, he chilled out though. That nigga only tried to beat on people he knew he could beat.

I continued to my mom's house, pushing almost a hundred on the highway. Thankfully, it wasn't a lot of traffic today because I didn't plan on slowing down.

————

"How could they be letting him out, Brady? Do they not know he will kill me?" My mom cried on my shoulder.

I wrapped my arms around her and gritted my teeth. "That nigga ain't gone hurt you again. Over my dead body will I let that happen. If he comes near you, I'm killing him."

I felt my mom's body tense up. "Brady, don't talk like that."

She pulled up and looked at me. I could tell by the look on her face that the words I just spoke worried her, but I wasn't taking that shit back. If that nigga had the balls to step to my mom, I was ending his life and dealing with the consequences later.

"I hate that I didn't leave before things got worse. It caused you to have rage and anger in you. The same anger and rage your father often had." She lowered her head.

"Don't compare me to that nigga. I'm nothing like him," I frowned. That was the worst thing someone could tell me was that I reminded them of my sperm donor. It was bad enough I used to get told I looked like the nigga. I never wanted to act like him.

"I've seen you angry, Brady. You get to the point just like your father. The only difference is you're better at controlling it. That's my fault though. I used to let him beat the both of us. I tried to stop him so many times, but I couldn't." My mom started crying again.

"Why didn't you just leave him?"

Reaching up to wipe her eyes, my mom stared at me with sad eyes. "Your father was all I knew. He isolated me from my family. I didn't have a lot of friends then. It was just me, you, and him. I loved him and I always thought the last time was the last time. He would tell me he was getting help and going to counseling for his anger. Like a fool, I believed him. I wanted my family, and I wanted him to get his shit together," she paused and closed her eyes.

"I remember when you were twelve. You were bouncing the basketball in the house, even though you weren't supposed to. You ended up losing control of it and it hit your dad. He chased you into your room and just kept hitting you with his belt. I ran into the room and tried to pull him off of you. He ended up giving me a concussion that night. You stayed out of school for a week after that. I'm sorry, Brady, you should have never had to go through that." My mom's cries grew louder.

I pulled her into me and hugged her tightly again. I remember the night she was talking about. After that, I stayed away from home for real. I was either at Lucas or Tariq's house, only coming home to sleep and wash my ass.

I hit a growth spurt soon after that. When I was fifteen, my dad thought he was going to keep beating my ass. I shocked that nigga when I fought his ass back. That stopped the beatings on both my mom and me, or so I thought.

Later I found out he was still hitting her when I was gone.

"That's the past. I ain't worried about that shit anymore. I'm worried about how that nigga getting out is going to affect you. I remember how you were when all that stuff first happened. Do you want to come stay with me?" I asked her.

My mom shook her head then looked at me. "I can't keep running from that man. Plus, I don't want to be a burden on you more than I already am. Your father doesn't know where I live and he's not allowed near me. As long as he doesn't know where I stay, I'm okay."

I didn't like that shit. Even though he didn't know where she stayed, I still didn't like the fact that she was here alone.

"I don't know if I like the fact that you're here alone."

"Brady, I'll be fine, baby. It just freaked me out hearing that he was getting out."

I stared at my mom. She was a beautiful woman. Didn't look a day over forty.

"Alright, I can't force you, but the offer stands." My mom grabbed my hands in between hers.

"I have news for you," I told her smiling, wanting to lighten up the mood.

She stared at me curiously. "What?"

"Renee's pregnant." My mom's face lit up and she squealed.

"Is she really? I was wondering when you were going to give me some grandkids. How far is she?"

I laughed as my mom shot questions off left and right. "Woman, chill. We just found out. She hasn't been to the doctor yet."

"I'm so excited! You better let me know soon as yall go to the doctor."

My mom kept going on about the baby, which I was expecting. She had hinted about wanting a grandchild a few times, so now that it was finally happening, she could get off my back.

Speaking of Renee, I had to give her a call. She had called me, but I was focused on getting to my mom, so I didn't answer.

———

I WALKED into Renee's house and went straight to her bedroom. I ended up staying the night at my mom's house last night to make sure she was cool. Even though she had calmed down about my dad, I knew she was still shaken up.

When I walked into the bedroom, Renee was sitting on the edge of her bed in a towel on her phone.

"You must have been waiting for me," I called out, startling her.

She grabbed her chest and mugged me. "You scared the shit out of me." She rolled her eyes and looked back at her phone.

I walked over to her, grabbed her face, and kissed her. "My bad, baby."

"How's your mom?" she asked, giving me her attention.

I sighed and grabbed the back of my neck. I was still trying to get a grip on my dad getting out. Every time I thought about that shit, I got pissed off.

"She's better. I managed to calm her down. I tried to get her to come stay with me, but she wasn't having it."

Renee's face fell. "I'm sorry they're letting your dad out."

I shook my head. "Yeah, me too. That nigga deserves to rot in prison." I licked my lips as I looked her over.

"What about you? How you feeling?" Renee gave me a soft smile.

"I'm good, especially now that my man is back." She stood up and I pulled her into me, kissing her again.

"You missed your nigga?"

Renee nodded. "I did."

I smirked. "I told my mom about the baby. She's excited."

Renee tensed up in my arms, which seemed to happen whenever I mentioned her being pregnant. It was like she wasn't trying to acknowledge the shit.

I grabbed her towel and pulled it open, then placed my hands on her stomach. "Why you always do that?" I asked her.

"Do what? Sssss," she moaned as I moved my hands down between her legs. She opened her legs, giving me easier access, and I ran my finger over her slit.

"Get all tense when I mention our baby. You don't want my baby, Renee?" I leaned forward and started to kiss on her neck.

"You know I do," she moaned.

I stuck my finger inside her and she jumped.

"You not acting like it. Let me know how you feeling." I kept kissing on her neck.

"I'm scared."

I pulled away and stared at her.

Bending down, I picked her up. Her legs went around my waist. I backed up and laid her on the bed while kissing her.

Her legs were still wrapped around me.

"We already talked about this. You have nothing to worry about. You said you trusted your man. You weren't lying, right?"

Renee shook her head. "Good. I want you to be happy about this baby just like I am." I bent down and kissed her stomach. It was flat when she was laying down, but when she was standing up, she had a small pouch.

"I am, Brady!" she cried when I threw her legs over my shoulders and attacked her pussy.

"You need to make an appointment too, baby."

She looked down at me and quickly nodded her head. "I will." Her hand went to my head and she tried to push it down. I chuckled and went back to kissing on her pussy.

I understood Renee's fears, but I needed her to get over them and get on board with the fact that she was about to bring our baby into the world.

CHAPTER 27

LUCAS

I YAWNED AND WALKED INTO MY HOUSE READY TO TAKE MY ASS to sleep. It was going on four in the morning and we had just shut the night down. I was supposed to go pull up on Alisha, but my ass wasn't even in the mood.

I walked further into my house and was about to walk upstairs when I heard something in my kitchen. My eyebrows knitted together.

I stepped off the stairs and headed into my kitchen. I didn't have my gun on me, but I didn't give a fuck about all that.

"What the fuck!" I yelled.

Naudia turned around holding her chest. "Why the hell would you sneak up on me like that?" she yelled.

"What the hell are you doing in my house, making you something to eat? What if I had my gun and would have shot your ass?

Naudia rolled her eyes. "I needed somewhere to stay," she said, then turned and went back to what she was doing.

I watched her for a minute before shaking my head. I was tired as shit and didn't have time to get into her and Tariq's business. I would question her in the morning.

"Make sure yo clean my damn kitchen up, Naudia," I told her, turning and walking away.

———

ONCE I WOKE up and handled my hygiene, I went to find my crazy ass sister to find out what was going on with her and Tariq. He wasn't really saying shit last night besides they got into it, but I knew my sister would tell me.

I found Naudia sitting in my living room with a full damn pizza in front of her.

"Damn you hungry?" I asked her, taking a seat next to her.

Naudia glanced at me for a minute before looking back at the TV. "You know I always eat when I'm stressed out."

I nodded and reached for a piece of pizza, causing her to give me a dirty stare, but I ignored her.

"What the hell happened with you and Tariq?"

Naudia looked down at the pizza in her hand before taking a big bite of it. She put it down on the plate next to her, then grabbed a paper towel and wiped her hands.

"He thinks I cheated on him." Her shoulders slumped over.

"Shit, did you?"

Her head whipped in my direction. "No! I don't even know why you guys would think that!"

"Then why does he think that, Naudi? Tariq has been my nigga forever, and I know he wouldn't just go off on some shit for no reason."

Naudia exhaled a deep breath. "He saw a hickey on my neck."

"Naudia the fuck you mean he saw a hickey? From who?"

"This guy Nick." I sat my pizza down.

"I thought you were past that shit!"

"I am!" she defended. "I can't believe you guys think that fucking low of me! I didn't cheat on Tariq, and if both of you would let me explain before jumping to conclusions, you would know that!" Naudia jumped up and stormed out of the living room.

I was about to go after her when my phone went off in my pocket. I pulled it out and saw it was Alisha.

"What's up, girl?" I asked her, leaning back on my couch.

She smiled into the camera. "Hey, you busy today?"

"Nah, not until later. What's up?"

"Well, since you bailed on me last night, I thought you could make it up to me."

I smirked. "Oh yeah? What you got in mind." My dick jumped thinking about being inside her.

"I don't know. Why don't we go to the mall or something?" I frowned.

Alisha's ass always wanted to go to the mall. I don't know if she thought I was about to trick on her ass or some shit, but I wasn't that nigga.

"I don't need your money if that's what you're thinking. I have a party I need to find something for and wanted to know if you would come with me to find something."

"Don't you have friends for that shit?"

She smacked her lips. "Yeah, but I wanted my man to come with me."

I ran my tongue over my bottom lip. "Oh, I'm yo man now?"

A childlike grin appeared on Alisha's face. "I mean, yeah, unless I'm reading into shit too deep."

I chuckled. One thing I liked about Alisha is she wasn't shy at all. She knew what she wanted and had no problem going for it. It's always been like that with her, even back when I first met her.

"Yeah alright, let me know when you're trying to go."

The grin on her face grew. "Okay, baby. Bye!" She blew me a kiss and hung up.

I shook my head then stood up, slipping my phone back into my pocket.

Making my way upstairs, I went to the room that Naudia was staying in and knocked on the door before walking into the room.

She was laying on her back with her *Air pods* in her ear staring at the ceiling.

I walked over to the bed and took a seat on the bed. "Naudia."

I knew her ass could hear me, but she was ignoring me. I shook her leg. "Naudia, I know yo stubborn ass can hear me."

She snatched the earbud out of her ear. "What, Lucas?" she spat.

"Aye girl, take that base out yo voice. I wanted to come in here and say my bad, alright. I shouldn't have jumped to conclusions like that."

"You're right, you shouldn't have. I know my past behaviors weren't the best, but I've changed. I thought yall could see that." A sad look appeared on her face.

I started to feel like shit. Naudia was right; besides the bullshit with school, she had done a complete three-sixty from how she used to be. From what I know, she wasn't out here sleeping around anymore or partying too much. She had been lowkey up Tariq's ass for real.

Ever since that shit happened to her and she got with Tariq, she's calmed down a lot. I gripped her leg. "You're right, I shouldn't have assumed anything. So what happened?" I wasn't trying to be in Naudia's and Tariq's business, but I didn't like to see my sister upset.

Naudia looked at me. "Just some bullshit. Tariq thinks I slept with Nick, but I didn't. He was kissing on me when I first got to his house. I'm not going to lie, at first, I got caught up in it, but it didn't last. I pushed him off then told him I was in a relationship and couldn't see him anymore. Obviously, I didn't push him off quick enough because he left a mark on my neck that Tariq pointed out." I nodded.

Shit, I didn't blame Tariq. If that was me, I would be pissed too. "So he kicked you out?"

Naudia shook her head. "No, but he told me he was done with me and left. I tried to call him, and he didn't answer. I wasn't about to stay anywhere I wasn't wanted."

"Naudia, do you not know anything about the nigga you're with?"

She stared at me confused. "Of course, I do."

"Then you know if he didn't want you there then he would have kicked yo ass out. If I know Tariq, he needed to calm down. You shouldn't have left."

"Why the hell would I stay at his house when he broke up with me?"

"Since when does your hardheaded ass listen to anyone?"

Naudia giggled. "This is different! I wasn't about to beg him to be with me."

"I'm not saying beg him, but you shouldn't have left until yall talked either. If you didn't do anything then you should have stayed to talk to him."

"You didn't see his face. I'm sure he didn't want to talk to me." She got that sad look on her face again.

"Look, I don't know what the hell you did to that nigga, but Tariq is feeling the hell out of yo ass. Seeing that shit pissed him off, but if he didn't tell you to leave his house, then I'm sure he just needs some time before he spoke to you again."

She grew quiet. "So I should go talk to him?"

I shrugged. "That's up to you, little sis. I have never known you to give up that easy." I stood up.

Naudia started laughing. "Whatever. You here giving me relationship advice but won't fix yours."

"I'm not in a relationship. I'm single." I winked at her then headed out the room.

"Trinity is seeing someone, and I think she likes him. I advise you to get it together before it's too late," Naudia called out.

I stopped and my mind went to the nigga my daughter saw on Facetime. "Trinity is single," I told her and proceeded out the room.

I walked to my bedroom and shut the door. Taking my phone, I went to Trinity's contact and called her.

"What, Lucas?"

"Damn, it's like that?" I frowned.

She rolled her eyes. "Yes, now what?"

"Have you ran into Trevor?" Ever since she told me she ran into him, I been looking for Trevor. I even tried to have Tariq's cousin track the nigga's number, but nothing came up locally.

"No, Lucas, I haven't." I stared at her and smiled. It looked like she was in one of my t-shirts and her hair was in a low ponytail. Still, she looked good.

"Where's my baby?"

"Sleep."

I nodded. "Someone is calling me. I'll have her call you when she gets up."

I frowned. "Who you rushing off the phone for, Tri?"

"None of your business." She hung the phone up.

I stared at it in disbelief.

Yeah, I was mad at Trevor and Trinity, and I could admit I had been giving her a hard time since I found out, but I didn't expect her to move on so quickly. Part of me wanted to call her back to curse her out for hanging up on me. Just when I was about to, Alisha texted me.

Seeing that she wanted to meet up in an hour, I decided to say forget Trinity and get dressed. I'd handle Trinity another time.

CHAPTER 28

NAUDIA

I sat in my car and cursed under my breath seeing Tariq's car in his driveway. It had been three days since our fight, and I hadn't talked to or seen him since he walked out.

I wanted to take Lucas's advice to talk to him, but then I said fuck that. I wasn't the one in the wrong. I didn't do anything. If anything, Tariq should have reached out to me.

I had some stuff here I needed to get and take to my brother's house. The rest of my belongings from my house had been put in storage. I was happy I didn't get rid of it since it looked like I would be getting my own place again after all.

After giving myself a pep talk, I got out of the car and headed for the front door. I knocked on it and waited for a few minutes. Seeing that he wasn't going to answer, I smacked my lips and used my key to open the door.

I walked through the house and didn't see Tariq anywhere. Just that quick, I grew upset though. I already missed being here with Tariq.

I headed for the stairs and up to his room, hoping that he wouldn't say anything to me while I grabbed my stuff.

When I got into his room, I heard the shower running. I looked at the bathroom door and noticed the door slightly open.

Good, he was in the shower. That means I could grab my stuff and leave without seeing him. I walked to the closet and grabbed some of the bags I had left here. Since I thought Tariq would have reached out to me by now, I didn't take everything with me, but I was wrong.

I looked around the closet, picking up some of my clothes surrounding the bags. I loved Tariq's closet. It was a two-sided walk-in.

I looked over and frowned, noticing Chyna's stuff was still in here. I was tempted to take that shit and throw it away, but I thought against it. Tariq wasn't even mine anymore.

I took my stuff off the hangers and put it in my bags.

Picking the bags up, I walked out of the closet and froze in place. Tariq was staring right at me. He was rubbing a towel over his beard then dropped it to the floor.

My eyes instantly roamed to his well-chiseled body; my pussy started to throb, looking at his dick print in the towel around his waist.

"I'll take these to my car then come get the last two bags," I told him.

He pulled on his beard while his eyes pierced into me. They were that dark gray they normally got when he was upset.

"Where you going?" he finally asked me.

"Lucas's house until I find my own."

Still pulling on his beard, Tariq nodded. "So that's it? You moving out?"

I stared at him confused. "You broke up with me. I thought you would want me to leave."

Tariq crossed his arms. "Did I tell you I wanted you to leave?"

Slowly I shook my head. "You broke up with me though."

"Did I?" He paused with his eyebrow raised. "I just recall

telling you I was cool on this shit. I never said I wanted to break up."

"You walked out on me even when I told you I didn't do anything."

"Because I was pissed off. I was saying some crazy shit to you and left before saying some shit I couldn't take back. You're the one who left and stayed gone."

I was quiet. "I didn't think you wanted me here anymore," I told him lowly.

I shamelessly looked him over again. Just by him standing there I was getting turned on. Tariq had that aura though. He could be doing something simple as sleeping, and I would be ready to attack him. It was like my body couldn't get enough of him.

These last few days without him had been torture for me. I had become accustomed to falling asleep in his arms every night.

"Come here, Naudi!" he demanded, licking his lips.

I dropped my bags and slowly made my way to him. The whole time I kept eye contact with him, but my heart was beating quickly.

Tariq gripped my chin and intensely stared at me. "Did you fuck that nigga?"

I rolled my eyes and went to snatch away, but he held me tighter. "I already told you I didn't fuck him!"

"That's your word."

"Yes, Tariq! Damn, I wouldn't lie."

He nodded. "If I find out anything different, it ain't gone end pretty for either of you." His eyes grew darker. A chill shot through my body.

"You won't."

Tariq let my chin go and nodded. "So you leaving me, huh? We get into an argument and you go running?"

"Nigga you walked out on me! What did you think I was supposed to stay here looking stupid?"

"Shit, I thought you would be here when I got back ready to explain or some shit."

"I already did explain. What else did you want?"

"I wasn't in the right mind to hear that shit." He reached up and pulled on the end of my braids.

"You went back to the braids."

"Yeah, well," I shrugged.

"I shouldn't have blown up on you like that. You told me you didn't fuck that nigga and I should have believed you."

"Tariq, I thought that we were in a place where you didn't have any doubts when it came to me, but obviously, you still have some ill feelings from how I used to act. I don't want you thinking I'm out here hoeing around or something when I'm not around you."

"Naudia, I'm not some insecure nigga. I knew you used to fuck that Nick dude and that shit pissed me off thinking about you and him still fucking behind my back. I know how you used to be. Shit, I saw that shit first hand, but I'm not going to hold that against you. I knew what I was signing up for." Tariq grabbed my waist and pulled me forward.

"All that matters is that you're mine and all that shit is in the past." I stared up at him and my heartbeat sped up again.

Tariq always pulled these emotions out of me that I wasn't used to. Being that I never been in a serious relationship for real, this was new to me. Me caring what a nigga thought about me or me wanting his approval was foreign to me. It was almost like I was scared I would disappoint him in a sense.

Tariq always seemed to try to find the good in me even when no one else did. He was always so passionate about everything, and that's one thing I loved.

Shit. My hands grew sweaty while my mouth grew dry.

"I love you, Tariq," I blurted out.

My heart was about to beat out my chest. I wasn't sure how he would receive the news. I didn't know if it was too soon to tell him. All I knew was that Tariq made my stomach flutter every time he looked at me. That warm, fuzzy feeling those sappy movies always talked about happened in me every time he touched me. When his lips would touch me, it felt like I was being electrocuted and a shock went through my body.

When he didn't answer, I started rambling. "I don't know if you feel the same way or not, but I know it's real. It may be too soon, but I don't care; I know how I feel. You make me happy, almost like I'm floating. When you walked away from me that day, I felt like my heart was being ripped out. Like I couldn't breathe. Even being away from you for these three days was too long for me. I don't want to be apart from you. Tariq I-" he shut me up by my kissing me.

His tongue slid in my mouth and I moaned against his mouth. I could feel his dick starting to rise and it was currently poking the bottom of my stomach.

"You talk too damn much," he chuckled. "I love you too."

A smile formed on my face. "Do you really?"

"I do. Let me show you how much."

Tariq grabbed my hand and walked me over to his bed. Before he could tell me to get on the bed, I dropped down to my knees and removed the towel off his waist. I licked his large mushroom head. Circling my tongue around it. When I noticed the pre-cum oozing out, I looked up at Tariq. He stared down at me lustfully.

I grabbed his dick and lifted it, running my tongue under it up to the top then licking the pre-cum off before taking him in my mouth. I sucked Tariq's dick like I was trying to win a prize. He started humping my face, which turned me on even more.

Sloppily, I sucked on his dick while rotating my hands around it.

"Shit, Naudi!" Tariq groaned. I glanced up. His eyes were closed, and his head was back.

My mouth grew wetter and I took him to the back of my throat. Humming on his dick, I started massaging his balls. I felt the main vein in his dick throb. That caused me to suck harder. Soon Tariq was cumming down my throat. I made sure to continue sucking until he was done. I circled his dick one last time with my tongue before standing up.

Tariq stared at me in awe before pushing me on the bed. He climbed on top of me, staring into my eyes. "Watching you suck my dick is sexy as fuck." He kissed me passionately.

Tariq quickly pulled me up and stripped me from my clothes. I squirmed as he held my thighs open and kissed the inside of them.

"Riq!" I panted.

Sucking his dick already had made me horny. I don't think I could take foreplay. My pussy was leaking, and he barely even touched me.

"I could feel the heat coming off your pussy Naudi. She ready for me, baby?"

"She's ready," I cried. Tariq continued to kiss the inside of my thighs, every so often biting them.

My breathing sped up. Tariq's mouth got closer to my pussy. I could feel his warm breath brushing against it. My leg jerked.

"You getting excited already," he chuckled.

"Baby, I can't handle it."

"You can't?" He brushed my pussy with his fingers.

I bit down on my bottom lip and shook my head. "Damn she's wet as fuck. This all for me?"

"Only you, baby." Tariq gave me a lop-sided grin then kissed my pussy a few times. He spread my pussy and started licking on my clit. My head went back, loving the feeling of his mouth on me.

His fingers started moving in and out of me while he continued to kiss and suck on my clit. My legs started twitching and I was struggling to keep them open. My eyes squeezed closed and my stomach tightened.

Tariq started thumbing my clit and sucking on it at the same time. "Riq!" I yelled, grabbing his head.

My eyes rolled to the back of my head as I came in his mouth. Tariq made sure to suck all my juices up to.

He kissed the top of my pussy, making his way up my stomach. I was breathing hard. While he kissed his way up my body, I tried to regulate my breathing. Tariq sucked on my nipples when he got to my breasts. His tongue went over my nipple, fast, wet, and quick.

My body started heating up again. Tariq gently pulled on my nipple with his teeth while massaging the other.

"Tariq, please," I begged.

I couldn't take it anymore. I needed him inside me now.

"What you want, baby?" He continued kissing up my chest.

"I want you inside me. Please, I can't take it anymore."

Tariq kissed his way up to my lips and connected his with mine. He sucked on my tongue. I gasped when he entered me. He pushed deep inside me, still kissing me deeply.

My legs spread wider as I accepted all of him. Tariq's strokes were slow and deep. He pulled slightly out before pushing into me. My back instantly arched.

"How that feel, baby? That's what you wanted?" he asked, moving down to my neck and biting on it.

I squeezed my eyes shut, loving the way he was feeling inside of me. "I love it, Tariq!" I yelled when his dick went deeper in me.

I started throwing my body against him. The way Tariq was handling my body was unfamiliar. His strokes were so slow and calculated. Every time he thrust into me, I could feel something spark inside of me. It was like my body was connecting to his.

Tariq grabbed my hands and intertwined his fingers with mine. He lifted them above my head and lifted his head, staring at me.

"You sure you love me, Naudia?" he asked me.

His strokes sped up some. "Yes, I do."

"You won't leave me again?" Tariq pulled his dick out so only the tip was in, then thrust the whole thing back in me.

My breath got caught and I quickly shook my head. "No, baby."

"You promise?"

I nodded. "I promise, Tariq. I love you. Shit!" I yelled as my body shook.

"Don't close your eyes. I want to see you cum, baby." Tariq let go of my hands and used one of his to grip my neck. He pulled up and started moving in and out of me faster.

I bit down on my bottom lip. "I love you, Naudia. I can't lose you; I don't want to lose you. You better not ever leave me." I went to answer, but my words got caught in my throat.

Tariq had my body feeling so good. He was fucking me like he was trying to stamp his damn name on my pussy.

"I'm not, Riq. I'm yours, baby." He gripped my neck tighter, my pussy got wetter.

"Only mine?"

"Only yours!" Tariq let go of my neck and bent down and kissed me again.

His hands went to my breasts and he massaged them. "Fuck, Naudia! I can't pull out, baby," he said against my mouth.

"Don't," I begged, wrapping my legs around him.

Right now I felt so connected to Tariq that I was ready to have his kids with no hesitations. I never wanted to lose him.

Tariq was soon cumming inside me and I came again too.

He laid on me, still kissing me and holding me.

"You're not going back to your brother's," he finally said.

I took a few deep breaths. "Trust me, after this, I wasn't planning on it." Tariq wiped some of the sweat off my forehead then rolled off me.

My eyes grew heavy as I continued to lay there. My pussy was still pulsating, and I knew I needed to go clean up, but I couldn't move.

I jumped when I felt something wet between my legs. I looked down and Tariq was wiping between my legs.

Soon he was back in bed with me. He laid behind me and pulled me into him.

A smile graced my face as I drifted off to sleep. Tariq was about to turn on a different set of emotions in me. I hoped he was ready.

CHAPTER 29

TRINITY

"MOMMY!" LUCIA CALLED OUT FROM THE BACKSEAT.

"Yeah, baby?" I asked, turning onto Lucas's street.

"Do you and daddy hate each other?" My eyes widened hearing her ask me something like that. I was taken aback by her question. I know me and Lucas weren't together, but I didn't see where she would get that we hated each other.

I pulled into Lucas's driveway and put my car in park. Undoing my seat belt, I turned to look at Lucia and smiled at her. She had her *iPad* in her lap but was staring directly at me.

"Why would you ask that, Lucia?"

Her small shoulders rose then fell. "My friend at school said her mommy and daddy hate each other that's why they don't live together. We don't live with daddy anymore."

My mouth slightly opened. "Lucia, me and your father don't hate each other."

"Then why don't we live with him anymore?"

I sighed, trying to put this so that she would easily understand. "Sometimes people just need space from each other. Me and your dad love each other, we always will."

"Well, then can we live with daddy again?"

"You miss living with your dad?"

Lucia nodded her head. "I miss my old room too."

"You don't like our new house?"

"Yeah, but daddy's not there. He doesn't come in my room to kiss me at night anymore when he thought I was sleeping."

I stared at her shocked. "He used to come in your room?"

Again she nodded. "I would hear him. He would wake me up, but I kept my eyes closed. He kissed me and told me he loved me every night."

That was news to me. When Lucas used to come in late, I used to get upset because he was missing time with his daughter. Even though that still bothered me, he was making a much better effort with her, making more time for sure. It warmed my heart knowing he would go in and kiss her whenever he came home.

"Me and your dad have to work out some things before we decide if we're going to be back together."

"But aren't we a family?"

"Of course, we are, baby."

"Then shouldn't we all live together?" I had to smile to stop myself from crying. Lucia was such a smart, observant little girl.

"Just because we don't live together doesn't mean we aren't a family. As long as we love each other, we're good." Lucia stared at me then at our old house.

"I still want us to move back with daddy!" She finally opened her door and ran to the door.

I watched Lucia bang on the door and a smile graced her face when Lucas finally opened the door. She hugged his waist then rushed into the house.

Lucas closed his door then walked over to my car. I took a deep breath preparing myself. Nowadays, I wasn't sure how our interactions were going to go.

I rolled my window down. He put his arms on the top of the car and leaned over.

"What's up?" he asked me.

"Hi, Lucas." I looked up at him.

He stared down at me. "So where you going?"

"Lucas," I sighed. I wasn't trying to do this with him right now. It's like all he wanted to do was argue with me.

"Damn, I can't ask you a question? You call asking if you can drop our daughter off and I can't ask why?"

"If it's a problem, I can call my mother or Naudia to keep her."

Lucas's face turned. "I never fucking said it was a problem. It's never a problem for my daughter to come with me, Trinity. Where you going dressed like that?"

I looked down. I had on a red dress; it was cut a little low in the front with a slit on the side.

"I'm going on a date, Lucas," I finally told him. I knew he wouldn't let up until I told him.

His tongue ran over his top teeth. I thought he was about to act a fool, but to my surprise, he didn't. Lucas nodded his head then stepped back.

"Alright, be safe. I'll call you when I'm dropping Lucia off. I'll probably keep her for a few days."

I squinted my eyebrows together. "That's it?"

"Yep, enjoy your night." He turned and headed to the house. I sat there kind of lost. That wasn't the reaction I was expecting. Actually, it was nothing like Lucas at all. A part of me was hoping he would show his ass. At least then I'd know he still gave a fuck about me.

Lucia's words played over in my head, which put a damper on my mood. Here I was telling her that Lucas and I still loved each other, but the way he just acted, I wasn't sure if it was just a one-sided thing now.

———

"Everything okay?" Myles asked, looking over at me.

I lifted my eyes from my food to meet his eyes. Forcing a smile on my face, I slowly nodded.

"Yeah, I'm sorry, I just have a lot on my mind right now," I confessed.

I hated that Lucia's words and Lucas's actions were weighing heavily on me. It had me second-guessing if being out with Myles was the right thing. Yes, I was single, but I wasn't over Lucas. I still wanted my family, but I wanted Lucas to forgive me and take our relationship more seriously. I spent so many years allowing him to walk all over me and he got comfortable with that.

"Trinity?"

I shook my head. "I'm sorry, what?"

Myles smiled then reached over and grabbed my hand. "I asked what was on your mind, beautiful?"

Bashfully, I smiled at him. Myles was such a sweetheart. He was the complete opposite of Lucas in every way when it came to personality.

"Just something my daughter said to me."

"Which was?"

I sighed and licked my lips. "She told me she missed me and her dad being a family." My shoulders dropped.

One reason I left Lucas is that I wanted him to be a better father. I didn't want to see my daughter hurt, but it seemed to be the outcome anyway.

Myles squeezed my hand. "And do you miss that too?"

I stared at him, not sure how to answer. Lifting my other hand, I brushed a piece of hair out of my eye.

"You can be honest with me."

"I do. We were together for damn near a decade. He's all I know. I also know I couldn't keep allowing him to walk all over me either. I'm confused, I guess." I expected Myles to look upset, but he didn't.

"I get it. It's hard to get over someone quickly with that much history. I like you, Trinity. You seem like a great girl, but I'm not trying to be a rebound or pressure you into anything either."

"I'm sorry. I shouldn't have been trying to date when I wasn't fully over him." I shook my head.

"Nah, don't apologize. Your ex is a fool to let you go and allow someone to come in and take his place. I'm cool with us being friends for now. I want you to handle any open feelings you have before we try to go further."

Slowly a smile appeared on my face. "Myles, you're such a great guy."

He licked his lips. "Well, you seem worth the wait." I giggled.

Myles bit down on his bottom lip.

We finished our dinner while eating and talking about little things, getting to know each other more.

Myles held my hand and led me to my car. When we reached it, he grabbed my waist and looked down at me.

"I had a good time with you," he said lowly.

The way he was staring at me had my body heating up. I hadn't had sex in a long time, and I was overdue.

"I had a good time too." Myles leaned down and kissed me.

It was the first time we kissed, and it seemed to wake my body up. I gripped the bottom of his shirt as our kiss deepened.

"I don't want tonight to end," he said, kissing me again.

"Me neither," I panted.

"Follow me back to my house?" Myles pulled up and stared at me.

Slowly, I nodded my head. He pecked my lips a few more times before pulling back and opening my door.

When I slid in the car, he went to his.

I sat there while my heart raced. Besides Trevor, I had never been with another guy outside of Lucas, but I was trying not to think of that. He was out here sleeping with Alisha and whoever else, so why should I be lonely and sexless?

———

I GRIPPED the sheets tightly and arched my back as Myles sucked on my pussy. My legs begin to twitch, and my stomach clenched.

"Shit!" I yelled, throwing my head back with my eyes shut.

Soon as we got to his house, he took me right to his room and was on me. He started kissing all down my body as he stripped me out of my clothes.

"Your pussy taste so good, baby," he said, sloppily kissing my lower lips. He had two fingers moving in and out of me. His fingers pushed deep inside of me and he pulled on my clit.

"Myles!" I yelled as I started cumming. He grabbed my bottom half and lifted it up, digging his face deeper into my pussy. His tongue ran lower, and I jumped when I felt it graze my ass.

"Wait, wait!" I panted, trying to push his head away. Myles ignored my pleading and continued as he was.

I gripped his sheets again when I started cumming for the second time.

Myles sucked my juices and stood up. I laid on his bed breathing heavily, watching him. He smirked down at me and licked my juices off his lips

He walked over to his dresser and opened it. I saw him take a condom out. Using his teeth, he ripped it open and walked back to the bed. Still standing up, he grabbed my legs and yanked me to the edge.

Myles stared down at me as he placed my legs on his shoulders. I felt his dick against my lips. Myles held his dick and tapped my clit with it. My eyes closed as he rubbed his dick up and down my pussy.

"Just put it in," I begged.

Myles finally pushed his dick inside me. My breath caught as he filled me.

Myles wasn't small, and he was actually giving Lucas a run for his money. The only thing Lucas had on him was width, but Myles was filling my walls nicely.

Myles held my thighs and started moving in and out of me. His hands moved down then up to my chest. He squeezed my breasts then took my nipples between his hands.

I lifted my body against his to fuck him back.

"Damn Tri, this pussy feels so good," Myles mumbled.

Hearing him call me Tri caused me to tense up slightly. Myles pushed his dick deeper inside me.

"Fuck!" I yelled.

Leaning forward, Myles took my nipple in his mouth, never missing a stroke. Soon I was cumming. Myles let my legs go and pulled out of me.

"Turn around."

I opened my eyes and stared at him like he was crazy. He grinned, then grabbed me, flipping me over.

His dick pushed back inside of me. He gripped my hips and started pulling my body back against him. I dug my face into the bed and started throwing my ass back.

After a few minutes of going at it, we finally both ended up cumming.

I collapsed forward on the bed and closed my eyes.

Myles hovered over me and kissed my back.

"I'm not done with you yet." He flipped me over. I opened my eyes and his mouth connected with mine. I could feel him growing under me.

Even though we were taking things slow, I was happily willing to accept his good dick.

CHAPTER 30

RENEE

"You ready for tonight?" Brady asked me, dropping his towel.

Briefly, I got caught up staring at his dick resting near his thigh. Even when soft Brady had a nice size dick. I should be tired because we been having sex all damn morning, but it was like this pregnancy had kicked my sex drive into overtime. Even though sex had gotten a lot more uncomfortable for me, I still wanted it whenever I was near Brady.

"Renee, you gone keep staring at my dick or answer me?" I snatched my eyes up to meet his.

"Oh yeah, I guess it's now or never," I shrugged, sitting on his bed.

Tonight we were telling our friends about my pregnancy. Well, I was telling my friends that is. Brady told me how he told his friends already. Even though I wanted him to wait, I wasn't mad. I was starting to accept my pregnancy.

I've only had a few days where I experienced morning sickness. The main thing that seemed to be happening was my weight gain. Since I confirmed my pregnancy, it was like the weight's been coming fast. Brady said I was imagining it, but I knew I wasn't. I had already gone up two pants sizes in the past month.

I picked up the dress next to me that I decided to wear today. We decided on a simple gathering. Brady had thrown a few things on the grill, and we had set up his backyard so our friends could come over and eat.

Brady came and stood in front of me, fully dressed now. "I still can't believe you're about to have my baby." He reached his hand out. After I put the dress down, I reached up and grabbed his hand.

"I know it's still shocking to me." I smiled at the thought of carrying a piece of him. His hand traveled to my stomach and he slowly rubbed it.

"You think we gone have a boy or girl?" I stared down at his hand on my stomach.

"I don't know or really care, honestly. I just want my baby."

Brady moved his hand to my neck and cuffed it. Pulling my face forward, he kissed me. "And you will. A healthy baby at that." I smiled against his mouth and pulled on his bottom lip with my teeth. My body was starting to react to him touching me.

Slowly, I sucked on his bottom lip, moaning quietly in my mouth.

"Renee, we just went like four damn rounds. I don't know how much more you want from my dick," he chuckled and pulled away from me.

I bit down on my bottom lip and looked towards his center. "It's not my fault. It's this baby. It has me so horny," I whined.

Brady shook his head. "I need to go start the grill. Finish getting dressed and get sex off yo damn mind." I frowned as he turned and headed out of his bedroom.

Turning around, I picked my dress back up and went into the bathroom.

———

"It's nice all of us are getting together," Trinity said, sipping on the wine cooler Naudia had gotten from the store.

"Yeah, it is. I feel like we haven't just hung out since we were in Cancun," Naudia commented, sipping her wine cooler. She said she wasn't drinking hard anymore, so she was sticking to those for a while.

"It sucks the crew doesn't get together and hang out anymore. We always have a good time as a group."

I nodded then looked over to where the guys were. They were laughing and yelling about something while drinking whatever was in their cups.

"I know it feels like we all separated-" Trinity stopped talking and sat her wine cooler down. She reached into her pocket and took her phone out. My eyebrow raised when a huge smile appeared on her face.

"Hold on." She turned and walked off.

"What was up with that?" I asked Naudia staring at Trinity.

"I don't know, but I know that had to be a nigga that called her. You see how big she smiled?"

I looked over at Lucas. "So her and your brother are for real over then?"

Naudia shrugged. "It seems like it. Lucas says the Alisha girl he's seeing is just fun, but Trinity seems to really like the guy she's talking to."

"Yeah, her ass been around here smiling a lot lately too."

"It sucks it's not with my brother, but I'm happy for her."

Trinity walked back over to us, and both me and Naudia stared at her. "What?" she asked, grabbing her wine cooler.

"Don't what us! Who was that?" Naudia asked.

That goofy smile appeared on her face again. "Myles. The guy I been telling you two about."

"So things are going good with you two?" I asked.

Trinity slowly nodded her head. "Great actually. We've decided not to rush anything being that I just got out of a long relationship, but I'm enjoying us getting to know each other."

The way she said it had me side-eyeing her. "Bitch yall had sex?"

Bashfully, Trinity nodded her head. "Oh shit! How was it?" Naudia asked, getting excited.

Trinity took a deep breath. "Look, all Ima say is your brother is no slouch in the bedroom, sorry," Trinity laughed when Naudia twisted her face up. "But Myles is in another league. I don't know if it's because he's older, so he doesn't just want to fuck all the time. He takes his time with my body. I be ready to suck my damn thumb when we done."

Naudia and I looked at each other before both laughing. Trinity had never talked about another guy like this before. It was weird seeing it, but she looked like she meant it. She didn't look stressed out, and I was happy for my friend.

"Baby, come on, the food is done." Brady walked over to me and grabbed me.

Naudia and Trinity followed behind.

When we got to the table, I took a seat next to Brady. Tariq and Naudia sat next to each other, and Trinity and Lucas had no choice but to sit next to each other.

At first, none of us didn't really talked. Everyone was focusing on eating.

"Damn Renee, that's like your third set of ribs. You not full?" Naudia asked laughing.

I looked up from my plate and glared at her. "No, I'm not."

"Her ass is eating like she pregnant. She done loaded up on sides too," Trinity laughed.

I turned my glare to her. Looking down at my plate, I had to laugh to myself. I had been pigging out. This the first time I've eaten all day and I was taking full advantage of it.

"Because I am," I finally said and took another bite of my food.

Both Naudia and Renee stopped laughing and stared at me with their mouth dropped. "Wait, say that again."

Grabbing my napkin, I wiped my hands and grabbed Brady's hand. He gave it a small squeeze then reached over to kiss my cheek.

"I'm having, well, we're having a baby. I'm twelve weeks."

Last week I had finally went to see my doctor. Brady kept getting on me about putting it off, and I finally decided it was time for me to accept things. After I saw my baby on the sonogram machine, I fell in love. That was when it got real to me. Now I couldn't wait for it to get here.

"Shit Nae! That's so good! Congrats!" Naudia yelled. She rushed over to me and threw her arms around me, causing me to snicker.

"I know how excited you were to be a mom. I'm so happy for you!" she said, kissing my cheek.

"Thank you. I was scared at first, but I'm excited now." I looked over at Brady, who was grinning at me.

"Yeah, congrats Renee. It's about time someone else has a damn kid. I was tired of being the only mom. I felt so old," Trinity frowned.

All of us laughed. "So, Brady, you're excited?" Naudia asked him.

"Hell yeah. I can't wait to see her push my baby out." His arm was now wrapped around me.

"Man, nigga you don't want to see that shit. Do you know how much pussies stretch when a woman gives birth? When I watched Trinity birth Lucia, a nigga almost passed out."

"You did pass out!" Trinity turned to him and laughed.

He frowned down at her. "I thought we agreed not to tell anyone that."

"No, you agreed not to tell anyone," Trinity laughed harder, causing everyone to join in.

"Damn nigga, you went out like that. How come we didn't know that!" Tariq asked between laughs.

"Because it was supposed to be something that stayed in the delivery room."

"It's okay, baby daddy. It was only for like five minutes then you came back."

Lucas lifted his hand and playfully mushed her face. "Yeah alright, that shit was something crazy, but it was amazing to see. I loved watching her push our daughter out. I would love to see it again." He stared down at her. Trinity looked up at him. For a moment, the two of them stared at each other before she cleared her throat and turned her head.

"Yeah, Renee, birth is no joke, but I loved being pregnant." Lucas kept his eyes focused on Trinity while she kept trying to avoid his eye.

"Brady nigga you ready?" Tariq asked.

"Hell yeah. I wish I could speed this shit up." He pulled me into him, and I laid my head on his chest.

"This shit is wild. Renee and Brady are bringing a baby into the world." Naudia stared at the two of us.

"So I guess it's time for you to join the club next, huh sis," Trinity asked her.

Naudia's cheeks grew red. She looked up at Tariq and he smirked down at her. "We're not ready for that," she said quietly.

Tariq grabbed her into him and said something in her ear. Naudia's eyes widened. She pulled away and looked at him, then around the table, her cheeks seemed to grow redder.

"Yo ass better not end up pregnant no time soon." Lucas mugged her.

"Why can't she have a baby right now if she wants?" Trinity asked him.

"She's too young. She doesn't even have her life together."

"I was young and didn't have my life together either."

"Yeah, well that's different. It was meant for you to have my baby." He winked at her, and she rolled her eyes then lowered her head, trying to hide her smile.

"Anyway. This isn't about me having a baby. Renee, I know you and Brady will be great parents, and I can't wait to spoil him or her," Naudia jumped in and said.

We ended up having a good time. Surprisingly, Lucas and Trinity even were civilized. It felt like old times with us all together. I missed times like this. It was like ever since Trinity and Lucas broke up, we didn't all get together like we used to.

Towards the end of the night the guys left to get things ready at the gambling hall.

"So you really ready for this?" Trinity asked, sitting next to me.

"Yeah, are you?" Naudia sat across from us with her feet crossed.

I looked at both of them and thought about it.

"Honestly, I'm not. I'm scared as hell. When I first took the test, I wasn't even trying to entertain the thought of being pregnant. Yall remember what I went through, but Brady helped a lot of that. He assured me I had nothing to worry about and that he would be there for me. So I don't know, I'm scared, but I'm happy at the same time.

"Hell, I know that feeling. When I first found out I was pregnant, I was a nervous wreck. Lucas walked into my apartment to me balled up on the floor crying. He picked me up and carried me to my bed, sat me on his lap, and demanded I told him what was wrong. When I finally told him this nigga got to grinning all hard and smiling like he had won the lotto," Trinity paused, shaking her head.

"Moral of the story, I wasn't sure how things would play out. Lucas and I were so hot and cold. I had a part-time job, not really making a lot of money. On top of that, I didn't know shit about being a mom."

"But you love it now, right?" I asked her.

Trinity looked at me and smiled. "Hell yeah. Lucia is the best thing Lucas could have given me. Whenever I ask myself why I dealt with Lucas's shit for so long, I look at her, and it reminds me. If I didn't have both of them, I don't know how my life would have turned out. They changed me in so many ways, and I couldn't picture myself not being a mom now."

"Yeah, well I'm happy you're having a baby! I don't want kids anytime soon, but you're giving me another kid to spoil."

"I'm sure you and Tariq will be pregnant soon."

Naudia waved me off. "No, we won't. We are too new for kids for real. I want us to have some years in before we even think about bringing kids in."

"But you do want kids with him, right?"

"Yeah, eventually," she shrugged.

"Our Naudi is really growing up," Trinity gushed.

I laughed and nodded. "That she is."

"Whatever, I always wanted to have kids. I just realized that I want them with Tariq one day."

The three of us continued to talk until Trinity had to go pick up Lucia. Naudia stayed a little longer since Tariq wasn't going to be at his house for a while.

Now that my pregnancy was out there, I was even more excited to bring my baby into the world.

CHAPTER 31

LUCAS

"Quit playing," Alisha laughed as I kissed on the back of her neck.

"I told you to hurry and put some clothes on before I try and slide back into you." She giggled louder and used her elbow to push me away.

"Come on, we need to go find you something to wear." She turned around and wrapped her arms around my neck. Leaning up, she connected her lips with mine.

I had agreed to go to this party with her. I wasn't feeling it, but she kept begging me, so I said fuck it, it wasn't like I had anything else to do.

Alisha moaned in my mouth and my dick started to grow. I wrapped my hand around her and palmed her ass cheek.

"Let me slide in you one more time." I bent down and bit on her neck.

Pulling away from her, I looked her over before turning to get a condom out of my pocket.

———

"My dress is midnight blue, so we need to find you something to match it." Alisha looped her arm through mine.

I looked down at her. "What kind of party is this again?" I asked her.

"Well, it's not actually a party. It's her wedding."

I stopped walking. "Wedding?" I twisted my mouth out. "Alisha, I'm not trying to go to no damn wedding, especially around a group of niggas I don't know."

"But Lucas, you already said you would come."

"That's when I thought it was a party. I'm not feeling this shit."

She poked her lips out. "Please, my family is fun. I think you'll have a good time." Alisha leaned up and grabbed her face, then kissed me. She slid her tongue into my mouth, and I pulled on it with my mouth.

"What's me agreeing to go, going to get me?"

"Mhm, anything you want." She kissed me again then slid her hand down to where my dick was. I was wearing sweats, so her hand brushed against it.

"Daddy!" I heard behind me, causing me to break away from Alisha.

"Lucia, I told you not to take off like that!" I froze.

"But mommy, I saw daddy!" I stepped away from Alisha, who reached up and wiped my bottom lip.

"Daddy!" Lucia was now next to me.

"What's up baby!" I smiled looking down at her.

Bending down I scooped her up and kissed all on her face causing her to giggle.

"Daddy, stop," she laughed and hugged my neck. "Mommy, I told you that was him!" She turned to look at Trinity.

I hesitantly turned to look at her too. Instead of looking at me, her eyes were fixed on Alisha.

"What's up, Tri?"

Trinity forced her eyes away from Alisha to meet mine. "Hey," she said dryly.

I put Lucia down, but she stayed near me. "What are you doing here, daddy?" Lucia looked at Alisha and frowned. "Are you here with her?"

I looked over my shoulder at Alisha. You could tell she was uncomfortable. Making her way to me, she looped her arm in mine and smiled down at Lucia.

"Yes, he is. Hey, pretty girl."

Lucia looked behind her at Trinity then back at me. "Why are you with her?" It was crazy how much Lucia acted like my sister.

I licked my lips then looked at Trinity for help. She shrugged and took her phone out of her pocket. I sighed and moved Alisha's arm out of mine.

"This is Alisha, Daddy's friend. She came to the mall with me because I had to find something to wear."

Her frown deepened. "Why didn't you ask mommy and me to come?"

"Lucia, what did I tell you about questioning adults?" Trinity finally jumped in. I looked at her and nodded thanking her. She rolled her eyes then walked up to grab Lucia's hand.

"Come on, we have to go get your shoes."

"Wait, I want daddy to come."

"Daddy is with his friend. He can't come."

"But I want him to hang out with us."

"Lucia, please, not today."

"His friend can come."

"NO, she can't," Trinity's voice slightly elevated. "Just tell your dad bye and come on." She let Lucia go.

Lucia pouted then looked up at me. "Daddy, why can't you come with us?"

It broke my heart to see how sad Lucia looked. I looked behind me at Alisha, who was now on her phone.

I bent down so that I was at eye level with Lucia. "Let me drop my friend off, then I'll come to mommy's house and hang out with you."

Her face lit up. "Mommy too!"

I glanced up at Trinity, whose eyes were staring at me. "Yeah, baby girl. Mommy too." Lucia threw her arms around and hugged me tightly.

"I thought we were going to get something to eat after this?" Alisha complained.

"As you can see, what his daughter wants trumps you," Trinity snapped.

"I wasn't talking to you."

"I don't care if you were or weren't. You just heard him say he was spending time with his daughter, so I don't know why you would think your plans wouldn't be canceled."

"Trinity, you can lose the attitude. Like I said, I wasn't talking to you."

Seeing this was going left, I kissed Lucia's cheek then stood up. "Alright, yall not about to do this with my daughter right here," I told the both of them.

Alisha smacked her lips, and Trinity grabbed Lucia. "Whatever Lucas. Get your little booty calls in line."

"Bitch, what did you call me?"

I whipped around and glared at her. "Don't disrespect her, especially not when my daughter is right here."

Turning back around, I went into my pocket and took some money out of my wallet. "Here, get whatever you're getting for her."

"I got it."

"I didn't ask you if you did." I gave Trinity a look that told her not to fight me. She snatched the money from me then she and Lucia walked off.

"Bye, daddy! See you later!" Lucia yelled.

I smiled then waved at her.

Once they were gone, I took a deep breath then turned to look at Alisha. She was staring at me like she had an attitude.

"So we're not going out to eat?" she asked when we started walking.

"Did you or did you not just hear me tell my daughter I would come spend some time with her?"

Ever since Trinity and I separated, I made it my mission to be with Lucia as much as I could. If she wanted to see me, I would make it happen, even when I was supposed to be at the warehouse. Missing some days were worth seeing my baby girl happy.

"Well, why don't you go get her and she come with us?"

I looked at her like she was crazy. "Nah."

"Why not?"

"Because I'm not about to have just anyone around my daughter."

Alisha stopped walking. "I didn't think I was just anyone."

"To my daughter, you are. The only person she's ever seen me with is her mom. I'm not going to change that unless I'm serious with someone."

Alisha rolled her eyes. "I thought we were getting serious."

"Right now, we're chilling. I told you I wasn't trying to get into shit serious right now. Damn you being annoying as fuck," I told her and started walking.

Alisha mumbled something behind me, but I ignored her. I didn't care how she felt right now. Lucia's feelings were more important than hers and would always outweigh hers. If she couldn't accept that, then she could move on.

———

"I LOVE how she wanted you to come over, but she ends up falling asleep." I looked down at Lucia sleeping on my lap.

I had been over here for almost two hours. Trinity had cooked something light, and now the three of us were sitting in her living room watching movies.

"You know my baby can't hang," I laughed, then gently moved her off me so I could pick her up.

She hugged my neck as I carried her into her room. When I laid her down, she gripped my neck tighter when I went to pull away.

"Are you leaving?" she asked, fluttering her eyes open.

"Do you not want me to?"

She slowly shook her head. "I want you to stay with me and mommy." I licked my lips.

Bending down, I kissed her forehead. "I love you," I told her. She smiled, then let my neck go and turned to her side.

I walked back into the living room and Trinity was cleaning up. She was bent over picking something up. I walked over to her and slapped her ass, causing her to jump.

"Why would you do that!" she yelled, rubbing her ass cheeks.

"It was just out there." I shrugged.

Taking a seat on the couch, I placed my hand behind my head then leaned back with my eyes closed.

"What are you doing?"

"Lucia told me she wants me to stay with you and her." I opened my eyes when I noticed Trinity didn't reply.

"What?"

"Nothing, she mentioned it to me too a few times." Trinity looked around her living room. "She told me she missed us being a family."

My eyebrows furrowed together. "When?"

Trinity shrugged. "A few weeks ago."

"Why didn't you tell me?"

"For what, Lucas? We're over, and I've finally accepted it. There's no need to beat a dead horse."

"So we done done, huh?"

"I mean, yeah. You hate me, right?" I licked my lips, then tucked my bottom lip between my teeth and stared at her.

"Did I say I hated you?"

Trinity shifted her weight to the side. "I mean, you acted like it. This the first time you actually had a conversation with me like you don't."

I thought about her words. When I learned about Trevor and her, my ego took a huge hit. I wasn't trying to be bothered by Trinity at first. Hell, my ass wanted to hate her, but I couldn't hate her. No matter how much I tried.

Trinity was forever embedded in my heart. I wanted us to work out the shit we had going on, but I wasn't sure if I could fully get past her fucking my homie. I loved her though, and that wasn't going to change anytime soon.

Being without her for these past months showed me how fucked up I was when it came to our relationship. It was little shit she used to do that I missed, simple shit like just calling me asking me when I was coming home.

Just when I was about to reply, her phone started vibrating on the couch next to me. I glanced down at it and my jaw clenched.

My eyes went to hers and she looked like she saw a ghost.

"So you and that nigga serious, huh?" I asked.

I glanced back down on the phone. A picture had popped up of her laying in the bed with some nigga kissing her neck from behind. The way the picture was taken it was hard to see his face.

"Lucas," she started.

The phone stopped ringing then started again.

I stood up and stretched.

"It's all good, Trinity. If that nigga's making you happy, then I'm good."

"But I-" Once again, I stopped her.

"I'll come get Lucia tomorrow, alright?" I bent down and kissed her forehead.

She gave me a skeptical look but slowly nodded her head. I turned and started for her front door.

I know Trinity thought I was about to blow up on her, and a nigga lowkey wanted to, but I couldn't. I had put her through so much shit that I didn't want to hurt her anymore. If being with someone new was what made her happy, then I was gone let it rock, for now at least.

CHAPTER 32

TRINITY

I walked into my parents' house ready to get Lucia and go home. I had just got off work and I was ready to go home and get in bed. I had been working the past five days, and tomorrow I finally had a day off.

"Hey mom, where's my baby?" I asked, walking into the living room.

"In the backyard with your dad doing God knows what." I nodded and went towards the back of the house.

"Trinity, let me talk to you for a minute." I stopped walking then turned to face her.

"What's wrong?" I took a seat next to her.

"How much longer are you and Lucas going to keep this up?"

I stared at her confused. "Keep what up?"

"This so-called being broken up. Hasn't this been dragged out long enough?"

"Mom we are broken up. Where is this coming from?"

"Lucia mentioned how she saw her dad at the mall kissing another woman. Is this really where you two are now?"

I grew annoyed at Lucia running her mouth to my parents, but I wasn't shocked. Lucia told my mom everything, even when I told her not to. It still pissed me off that Lucia saw Lucas with Alisha and the fact that the bitch tried to act like she was more important than my daughter.

"Mom, I don't want to talk about this right now. I'm tired and just want to go lay down."

"If you had Lucas at home with you, you would have more help with your daughter. It's not fair that you're a single parent."

I sighed. "When Lucas was at home with us, I still felt like a single parent. You know what I went through with him."

"And he's been doing better now, right?" I nodded my head.

My parents didn't know anything about me sleeping with Trevor. They thought that Lucas and I weren't together because I wanted him to do better. That was still the case. Even though he was doing way better with Lucia, Lucas had given up on trying to work things out between us. He hasn't even mentioned us being together.

"As a father, yes, he has, but that doesn't mean it's time for me to take him back or that we need to be together. I went through a lot in my relationship with Lucas, and he hasn't shown me that he's over the games.

"You two have been together for years, and you have a child together. Don't you think that's more than enough reason to make it work? I know you still love him."

I looked down at my hands. "Of course, I still love him. I'll always love him."

"And don't you want to be with him?" I looked up at my mom. I wish she would just let it go, but I knew that was too good to be true. My mom was old school. She didn't believe in divorces and breakups. Since Lucas and I had been together so long, she thought we should have been married with another kid by now.

"I've been with Lucas since I was seventeen, mom. Of course,

I want to make it work with him. We had a family together, but things happened." I shrugged.

"Things that the two of you can't work out?" I was about to answer when there was a knock on the door. I stared at her curiously.

Without saying anything, my mom got up and went to the door. I sat there waiting for her to come back.

"I'm so happy you could stop by Lucas." My eyes darted up and soon landed on Lucas.

"Mom, what is this?" I looked at my mom.

She smiled at me and grabbed Lucas's hand leading him to the couch where I was sitting. He took a seat next to me, and my mom sat in the chair near us.

"I think it's time for you two to get over this fight you two are having and work it out." My mouth dropped open but no words came out.

I looked at Lucas out the side of my eye. He looked as thrown off as I was.

"Mom, this isn't your business," I stressed.

"You're right, but it's affecting my granddaughter, so that makes it my business."

"My daughter is fine!"

"She's not. You two are juggling her between two different houses. The child doesn't know if she's coming or going. Her whole life has been changed because you two can't work this out. Now Lucas Lucia told me how she saw you with some lady friend. She was confused about what was going on, and frankly, I am too. Why aren't you fighting harder for your family?"

I could feel Lucas's body shift next to me. "I can't fight for something that's not there." I turned to face him. He was giving my mom a blank stare.

"What do you mean? You and Trinity still love one another, right? I know that you two were having minor issues because you were putting work over her and Lucia, but you've fixed that, right?"

"Mom!"

"Yes ma'am. I've worked on that."

"So, I don't get the problem. Trinity, you want your family back, right?"

They both looked at me. I cleared my throat and ran my hands over my pants. "Your daughter is seeing someone else, Mrs. Austin. So regardless of if I want to work things out, she doesn't want that, and I have to accept it."

"Trinity, is that true?" My eyes went to my mom's. She looked disappointed.

"I have a friend, yes, but we're not technically together." I cut my eyes to Lucas.

"I don't get it. If you both want your family back, why not just stop this foolishness and make it work. I'm sure Lucas has learned his lesson, honey."

"Why can't we, Tri?" Lucas looked dead at me and asked. "I'm guessing you didn't tell your mom the reason we're still not together."

My eyes widened. I wasn't expecting Lucas to bring that up right now in front of my mom.

"Am I missing something?" My mom looked between me and Lucas.

"With all due respect, Mrs. Austin, as much as I would love to take the blame for me and Trinity not being together, I can't. I found out she did some things and hid them from me. Things I'm not sure if I can forgive. I love your daughter and I'll always love her, but I don't trust her. I don't know if we'll ever get to that point again. Right now, us co-parenting is what's best for everyone."

My heart literally felt like someone stabbed me in it and yanked the knife out. I don't know why but a small part of me was hoping that Lucas would come here and listen to my mom about us making it work. Now that we weren't at each other's necks all the time, it was easier to be around him.

Even though Myles was a good distraction, it didn't take away my feelings for Lucas.

"Well, what did you do, Trinity? I'm sure it wasn't that bad."

I swallowed hard. "I just did something stupid. Something really stupid."

Footsteps could be heard coming our way, and I let out a breath of relief when Lucia appeared.

"Daddy!" she yelled, running up to us.

Lucia ran straight to Lucas and jumped into his lap.

"Well, hello Lucia." She looked over at me and smiled widely.

"Hi mommy!"

My dad appeared and took a seat next to my mom. "Well, this is a pleasant surprise," he mentioned looking between me and Lucas.

"Isn't it? Don't they look like a beautiful family?" My mom smiled.

"Didn't I tell you to leave it alone," my dad scolded.

"I can't when my granddaughter is involved. Look how happy she looks with the two of them together." I glanced at Lucia, she and Lucas seemed to be in their own world.

"Mom, please just let it go. I get you're trying to help, but it's not helping."

"Because you two aren't trying. Do you think being with your dad was always a walk in the park? We went through our stuff, but we knew we loved each other at the end of the day, so we didn't let it keep us apart. Trinity, I'm sure whatever you did can be fixed."

I tucked my hands between my legs and took a deep breath. I glanced at Lucas and his attention had gone back to Lucia. I loved seeing the two of them interact. It always reminded me that no matter what me and Lucas went through, we did one thing right.

"Mom, please just let it go," I begged.

I didn't want to discuss the whole Trevor thing. I wanted to move on from it. I hadn't heard from him since he approached me with Lucia, which I was happy about. Lucas didn't bring it up every time we spoke now. I just wanted to leave it in the past.

"Alexa, leave her alone. You see whatever it is, is causing her to grow upset. It's none of your business for real." I sighed in relief when my dad finally interfered.

My mom looked at him then rolled her eyes. "I'm just trying to help. This young generation is so stubborn. I don't get how you can just throw your family away so easy."

"It wasn't easy!" I yelled, finally getting fed up. "Do you think it was easy leaving the man I been with since I was seventeen, the man I share a child with, the man I used to wake up to every day, the man I love! Do you think I enjoy hearing my daughter beg for her dad, only for him not to be right down the hall like she's used to? It's not easy, but I'm making it work because I have to. I don't need you telling me how fucked up my family is because I already know. I'm dealing with it. Now please, mom, mind your business."

"Lucas, please bring my daughter to the car." I stormed out of the living room and to my car.

My mom had hit a lot of nerves and she didn't know how to just leave well enough alone. She didn't understand what I battled with every day.

I got to my car and got inside. I rested my forehead on the steering wheel and closed my eyes. I promised myself I was done crying but right now I was having a moment.

My back door opened and closed.

I looked up when there was a tap on my window. Turning my car on, I rolled the window down and stared at Lucas.

"Are you okay?"

"I'm good. I just want to go home and get in my bed."

Lucas looked back at Lucia then back at me. "I didn't know that was why she was calling me over here."

I shook my head. "It's fine. I don't even want to deal with it right now."

He nodded. "Tri look, I shouldn't-"

"Forget it, Lucas. I just want to go home."

I knew what he was about to say, and frankly, I didn't want to hear it. He threw me under the bus and wanted to apologize for it, but I didn't want to hear it.

"Alright. I love you, Lucia. I'll be to get you in a few days, okay?"

"Okay, daddy!" she said behind me.

I rolled my eyes then rolled my window up. Right now I just wanted him away from me. Lucas took a step back from my car, giving me room to back up.

"Mommy, are you okay?" Lucia asked me.

I looked in my rearview mirror at her and smiled. "Yeah, baby I'm fine."

"Then why did you yell at grandma?"

"I was just upset, but I'm okay now."

Lucia smiled at me. "I love you, mommy."

"I love you too, baby."

Lucia was so oblivious to all the madness around her and I just hoped it stayed that way.

———

MYLES CAME up behind me and wrapped his arms around me. He started kissing on the back of my neck while looking in the mirror at me.

"You seem tense," he said against my skin.

I sighed and connected my eyes with his in the mirror.

"It's just been a long few days."

"Obviously, I wasn't working hard enough if you're still stressed out."

I giggled then turned around to look at him. "No, you worked me out just fine. I just have a lot on my mind."

Myles lifted me up and sat me on his bathroom counter. After wedging his way between my legs, he gripped my thighs then stared at me.

"What's up?"

I wasn't sure how much I wanted to share with him. I didn't want to seem like I was pillow talking with him, but he was the only one not tangled up in me and Lucas's mess. Everyone in my life was connected to him somehow, so it wasn't always easy to talk to them about how I was feeling.

The incident at my mom's house was still heavy on my mind. It had been a few days and I haven't talked to my mom since. Lucia was at her dad's house, and I hadn't really talked to him either.

"I don't think you really want to hear about it," I told him.

"If I didn't want to hear it, then I wouldn't have asked."

"It's just the same shit." My shoulders dropped. "My mom called herself having a mediation session with me and my daughter's dad, but it only seemed to make things worse. I got pissed off and stormed out of the house. Now I don't want to talk to either of them. I just wish she would have left it alone."

"I'm sure your mom just wanted to help."

"She did. My parents are old school, so she thought we could work it out. She doesn't realize that there's a lot in our relationship that I didn't share with them. We both hurt each other. Even though I was willing to make it work, he couldn't let it go, so I'm trying to move on."

Myles rubbed my legs and I looked at him. "Call me a hopeless romantic, but I believe if two people are meant to be together, then it'll happen. I tell you all the time you're a great girl and anyone who can't see that is an idiot." He leaned in and pecked my lips.

"I guess you're a smart one, huh?" My mouth turned upwards.

"I guess I am."

Myles was making the confusion I felt about Lucas harder. One part of me wanted to hold on to hope that we made it work, but a part of me was starting to like Myles and wanted to see where things would lead.

CHAPTER 33

BRADY

"WHAT YOU GOT PLANNED FOR TODAY?" I ASKED RENEE LOOKING up at her.

She shimmied her way into her jeans causing me to smile. Her stomach was forming at the bottom, showing off her pregnancy bump.

"I have to go up to my school to talk to an advisor about my upcoming semester. Since I'm pregnant, the original schedule I had planned won't work out."

"You don't want to take next semester off?"

She turned around and stared at me. "Why would I do that?"

I sat up and threw my legs over the bed. "I mean by the time the semester starts, you're going to be what, six months? Three months later you'll be due. Do you think you'll be able to handle school and a newborn?"

She was quiet for a second. "No, but I don't want to take off the whole semester. If anything, I might take two classes online, so I'll still be somewhat on track," I nodded.

"Whatever you decide I'm good with. I just don't want you to put a lot of pressure on yourself. It won't be horrible if you skip out this semester, but if you think you can handle both, then I'm good with that too." She smiled at me.

"I'll decide after I talk to the advisor." Standing up, I made my way to her and stood directly in front of her. I looked down at her, taking in her pregnancy glow.

"Pregnancy looks good on you."

She frowned. "You're saying that now. Wait until I get bigger and start looking like a damn whale."

I chuckled and rubbed her stomach. "Even if you start looking like a whale, I'll still think you're pretty as hell."

She playfully rolled her eyes. "Yeah yo ass better. I'm revealing my pregnancy to my sister and mom soon. I'm sure they'll want to meet you."

I smirked at her. Renee didn't talk about her family too much. I know she was close with her mom and sister before she moved. I knew they talked frequently, but she didn't see them as much as she would like. I've talked to them a few times on FaceTime when she would be on the phone with them.

"That's what's up. I know they'll be happy." I bent down to kiss her forehead.

"Yeah, they will be. My mom was super excited when I was pregnant the first time. This will be her first grandchild officially."

Renee got quiet for a moment. "I know she's going to lose her shit," she laughed softly.

Renee turned and headed to the dresser to grab a shirt. She stayed here so often now that I just cleared space for her. I was at the point where I wanted to suggest she just move in here. Since we found out she was pregnant, she was pretty much here all the time for real. Whenever I came home from the gambling hall, she was in my bed cuddled up with her body pillow.

I watched her from behind. Her hips had started to spread some already. Her ass grew too. It was juicier than before her pregnancy. I know she was complaining about gaining weight quickly, but I didn't see the problem. At first, I thought she was exaggerating, but now I see she had gotten chunky quickly. Still, I loved that shit.

I walked up on her and pushed myself against her behind. Wrapping my arms around her, I kissed the back of her neck.

"I love you," I said against her neck.

She laid her head back against my back with her eyes closed.

"I love you too." I held her a little longer before finally letting her go.

I needed to get ready to head out along with her. Tech was finally back in town and had an order ready for me. Tariq's cousin hadn't heard anything else when it came to the DEA undercover, so it looked like we might be in the clear for that. Still, I was keeping the order to a minimum until we found out exactly how deep we were.

———

I WALKED UP to the back door that led to the back entrance of Tech's shop. There was a small hallway that led to his office.

I was about to knock on the door when I saw it was slightly cracked open. I heard voices. My eyebrows knitted together, and my top lip curled up.

"We've been undercover for the past month and we have yet to see any pills being sold through their gambling hall. You're going to have to wear a wire so we can catch them red-handed."

"A wire? It's bad enough I'm fucking working with yall. Now yall want me to fully become a rat."

"That or you can go back to jail. You're getting a lighter sentence for helping us, but if you would like to serve the whole term, we can do that too."

My trigger finger began to itch. The whole time we have been trying to figure out who the snitch was in our operation and it turns out it was Tech.

"Fuck man, you're really putting my damn life at risk. Do yall know what will happen if anyone finds out I'm working with yall?"

"You think we give a fuck about that? Your ass should be lucky the DA agreed to give you a plea deal. If it were me, I would have locked your stupid ass up for the full sentence."

I bit down on my bottom lip and slowly made my way out the back hallway until I was back outside. I hurried to my car and went into my glove compartment to grab my gun. Just as I looked up, I saw the nigga who Tech was talking to walk out the back. I wasn't sure if he was the undercover, but I made sure to memorize his face in my head.

I waited for him to leave the parking lot before getting out of the car and making my way back into the building.

Tech's snake ass had given us up, and I'm not sure how long he been talking, but I know it was my fault we were in this situation, so I needed to be the one to fix it.

When I got back to the office door, I pushed the door open.

Tech looked at me with a wide grin. I wanted to punch that shit right off his face. Knowing that I had been working with a rat made my skin itch.

"Brady, it's nice to see you, my guy."

I stayed quiet and glared at him. I took a look around the office then looked back at Tech.

The smile on Tech's face slowly faded when he realized that I wasn't smiling back. "Everything alright?"

I stepped closer to the desk. "You know I thought we were making good money together," I said lowly.

I was trying to keep my anger under wraps, but it wasn't easy.

Tech now looked nervous. "We are," he nodded. His eyes widened when he finally saw the gun in my hand.

I licked my lips and grinned. "You know I never liked rat muthafuckas." I lifted my gun and pointed it at him.

Tech's eyes widened and his hands went up. "Whoa, Brady, what's going on?"

"The best way to get rid of a rat is to kill a rat!" I snarled then pulled the trigger.

CHAPTER 34

TARIQ

"Chyna quit fucking playing with me! Call me back when you get this!" I hung up the phone then tossed it on my dresser.

Dropping my head, I ran my hands over my head and released a deep sigh.

I was growing annoyed with this shit. Ever since Chyna texted me talking about her being pregnant, it's like she went ghost on me. I went by her house and it was empty. Her phone's been off since she texted me. It was like she disappeared.

I couldn't believe she would kill my fucking baby without talking to me. I knew I hurt her, and it was fucked up how I handled shit with her, but I didn't think she needed to kill my baby because of that. If anything, it was a choice we should have made together.

My bedroom door opened. My head stayed down but I heard Naudia moving around the room before finally standing in front of me.

"You okay?" she asked, gripping my shoulders and squeezing them.

I looked up at her. She forced her way between my legs then looked down at me concerned.

"Yeah, I'm good."

"You sure? You looked stressed?"

The frown on my face slowly turned up. Naudia was always worried about everyone around her. People could say what they wanted about her, but she was always down for those she cared about.

I wrapped my arms around her waist and pulled her down on my lap. Nuzzling my face in her neck I kissed it a few times then inhaled her scent.

"I'm good. Just some shit on my mind. I'll work it out though."

"Anything I can help you with?" She started rubbing the top of my head.

I gripped her waist tighter.

"No, you're good," I kissed her neck one last time before looking up.

"What you buy?" I asked, looking at the bags on the ground.

"Just a few clothes, nothing major." She smiled and ran her fingers through my beard.

She looked down at me with concern was still on her face. "You sure you're okay?"

I smiled at her. "Yeah girl, I'm good." I grabbed the back of her head and brought her face to mine so I could kiss her.

She giggled then grabbed my face to deepen our kiss.

"So I was thinking," she finally said.

I side-eyed her. "I don't know if I want to hear it."

She laughed again. "It's not bad." Naudia paused then stared at me for a minute. "Since I'm not in school anymore, I should find something productive to do with myself."

I nodded. "I agree."

She bit down on her bottom lip then grinned. "Why don't I work at the gambling hall?"

My eyes squinted. "I don't know about that shit, Naudia."

"Why?" she whined.

"You brother don't even like you up there like that."

"So what. I'm not asking my brother. I'm asking you. Lucas fired that hoe he was fucking, and yall fired the girl who was stealing from yall, so you have open spots, right?"

I licked my lips. "I don't know, man. I know that you've chilled out, but I don't know if I like the idea of you being there every night."

Naudia rolled her eyes and smacked her lips. "For real, Tariq? What's the worst that could happen? I could bartend or work the blackjack tables."

I thought about it. It wasn't the worse idea. "Let me talk to Brady and Lucas and see what they say."

"I guess that's cool," she pouted.

I chuckled and grabbed her chin so I could kiss her. "Your spoiled ass thinks you always have to get your way."

"I do," she grinned.

Naudia turned her body so that she was straddling me. My dick started to respond to her.

"Why don't we get a quickie in before I have to leave," I told her, moving my hand to her waist.

———

"IT LOOKS like it's about to storm, so make sure you be careful," I told Naudia.

"I will, I'm just going to get Lucia and take her to my brother."

I looked at the money on the desk. "Okay, I'll see you in a few."

"Bye. Love you."

"Love you too, baby." I hung up the phone and sighed.

I had been at the gambling hall for an hour, going over

numbers and separating the money for the three of us. I put mine in the duffle bag I planned on taking home to put in my safe at home. After making sure everything looked good, I put the extra money in the safe then put Lucas's and Brady's in their bags then stuck them in the safe too. I had got the starting money for tonight together too, so we would be ready for tonight.

After I finished sorting the money, I picked my phone up to attempt to call Chyna again. I had slid by her house one last time before coming here, but her house was sold now. I wasn't sure what the hell her problem was, but she was pissing a nigga off.

I locked the office up then headed out to the main floor. We were due to start setting up for the night soon, so I had to run home quickly and come right back to help out.

I made my way to my car and went to open my door when I heard my called.

I paused and shifted the duffle bag on my shoulder before turning around.

"I don't have any words for you, my nigga," I told Trevor as he approached me.

"Damn it's like that? What I do to you?"

I mugged him. "I don't fuck with disloyal niggas."

Trevor chuckled. "Lucas must still be in his feelings about me and Trinity." He shook his head.

"That shit was foul as fuck Trevor. Why the fuck would you fuck Trinity?"

"Shit, Lucas used to dog her out all the time. I didn't think he gave a fuck."

"I always knew you was a grimy nigga, but I didn't think you were that bad."

"Shit happens," he shrugged. "Where's Lucas at anyways?"

"Do I look like that niggas keeper? Plus, I don't think you want to see him."

"That nigga always wore his feelings on his sleeve. I see yall niggas doing good though." His eyes went to my duffle bag.

"Take yo ass on Trevor. The only reason why I ain't fucking you up is that I know Lucas wants you himself."

Trevor grinned then reached behind him. My eyes narrowed when he pulled a gun out and pointed at me.

I laughed. "Nigga am I supposed to be scared of a gun?"

"Yall niggas treat Lucas like he's some God or some shit. Always so loyal to him."

I narrowed my eyes. "I don't look at no nigga like he God. Lucas just ain't no snake ass nigga like you. Instead of you joining us, you chose to rob niggas. That's yo fault. Get that fucking gun out my face before I get pissed off."

"Give me the bag."

"Nigga fuck you. I ain't giving you shit."

"Want to bet?"

"Trevor. I'm giving you one last chance to get the fuck on. Don't pull no gun if you not gone use it."

He smirked.

POP!

POP!

My eyes widened and I looked down.

Blood started pouring out my chest and side. I dropped down to my knees as a burning sensation shot through me.

"Should have just given me the money. If you make it, tell Lucas's punk ass, I'm coming for him." I held my wounds as Trevor came and snatched the duffle bag.

My breathing grew shorter as I laid there bleeding out.

CHAPTER 35

LUCAS

"Thank you for coming!" Alisha said kissing me.

I looked down at her. "Yeah, don't ask me to do no shit like this again," I frowned causing her to laugh.

"Why do you always have to be so mean?"

"I'm not being mean. This shit just ain't my scene."

I looked around the hall that her cousin's reception was being held in.

"You act like it was a horrible experience or something. My family was nice."

"I still don't like this shit."

My phone went off. I went into my pocket to grab it.

I saw it was Naudia telling me she was about to go pick up Lucia and bring her to my house.

"Aye, my sister about to drop my daughter off, so I have to head out," I told Alisha, stepping away from her.

"Maybe I can come stay the night tonight," she suggested.

"Did you not just hear my daughter was about to come to my house?"

"What does that mean? She'll be sleep, right?"

"So the fuck what? We already talked about this shit. I'm not bringing no one that ain't her mom around her."

Alisha started pouting. "How are we going to get serious when you don't even want me around your daughter?"

"Who said I was trying to get serious right now?"

Alisha was starting to get beside herself. I don't know why she was all of a sudden pushing us being together so tough. I been told her I wasn't ready to be in anything serious again for a while. At first, she was cool with it but now she seemed to be thinking differently.

"Look, I don't have time to argue with you. I need to get home so I can get my daughter. I'll holla at you later."

I bent down and kissed her forehead then headed for the door.

I didn't know any of her family, so I wasn't about to say bye to any of them. Some of them stared at me as I walked through the hall, but I wasn't paying them any attention.

———

"Shit it's raining hard as hell," I mumbled, driving down the street.

It had taken me forty-five minutes to get home because of the rain.

My phone went off and I hit my steering wheel to answer it.

"What's up Naudi?"

"Hey, I just got to Trinity's house. I'm just making sure you were home."

"Yeah, I'm about to turn onto my street now."

"Okay, I'll be there soon."

"Bet. Be careful, it's raining hard as hell out here."

"I know, I will." We hung up and I was at the light that was right before my street. I tapped my finger against the steering wheel.

I looked down at my middle console for my phone and didn't see it. I looked down and saw it had fallen.

Quickly undoing my seat belt, I bent down and picked it up.

When I sat back up, I saw the light had turned green. I tossed my phone into my lap and started going.

Just as I was turning onto my street, a bright set of lights came rushing at me. My eyes widened and I attempted to turn my wheel to avoid the car.

BOOM!

CHAPTER 36

NAUDIA

"THANK YOU FOR TAKING HER," TRINITY TOLD ME AS WE WAITED for Lucia to come downstairs.

"Girl it's no problem. I love my baby."

I stared at Trinity. "What you got planned?"

She shrugged. "Nothing. I'm about to lay down with some wine in my bed."

"No new boo tonight?"

She shook her head. "Girl, no. He has to work tonight so it's just me and my wine."

"Well, I hope that I get to meet him soon." I rolled my eyes.

"Well, I didn't think you wanted to meet him with how things are with me and your brother."

"Girl, that has nothing to do with me. Plus, I don't think you and Lucas are done for real."

Trinity laughed. "You're crazy."

I laughed along with her. "I do want to meet him though." She nodded.

"Okay, we can make that happen if you really want to."

We continued talking until Lucia finally came downstairs.

"Dang girl, I thought I was going to have to leave you."

"I couldn't find my rainboots."

I looked down at them. "That's why I told you to get them out before Naudia showed up."

Trinity walked over to Lucia and hugged her. "I'll see you in a few days." Trinity kissed her forehead.

She pulled back and zipped Lucia's coat up and tightened her hood.

"Bye sis," I told her, grabbing Lucia's bag then her hand.

"Hurry up and run to the car," I told her while tightening my hood and unlocking the door.

We took off running to my car. Lucia thought it was fun running in the rain, but my ass couldn't wait to get out of it.

"Tomorrow, can I stay at your house with you and Uncle Riq?" Lucia asked from the backseat.

I glanced at her in the mirror.

"Sure, I think your dad has to work for real. We can have a girl's night."

I pulled my phone out and called Lucas, but his phone just rung.

"I hope his ass is waiting at the door," I mumbled.

I continued driving and making small talk with Lucia.

"TT?" she asked.

"Yeah, baby?" My face balled up noticing all the traffic near Lucas's house. I could see the flashing lights in the distance.

Must be an accident.

"Why don't my mommy and daddy want to live together anymore?"

I looked in the mirror at Lucia and she had a sad expression on her face.

"Lucia, I think you should talk to your mom or dad."

She sighed. "I talked to mommy and she said her and daddy need a break, but I miss us living together." Sadness sounded from her voice.

Just when I was about to answer, I noticed something that caused me to slam down on my breaks.

"Lucia, stay in the car!" I yelled, snatching my door open.

I yanked my seat belt off and jumped out of the car.

"TT!" Lucia yelled.

I rushed to the area the officers were blocking off.

"Ma'am, you can't come over here."

"That's my brother's car!" I yelled, staring at Lucas's car.

The rain poured down on my body, but I ignored it. Lucas's car was barely noticeable. It was caved in and two of the tires had come off.

"We still need you to stay back."

"IS HE OKAY!" I yelled, trying to run around the officer, but he grabbed me. My heart started beating faster and tears clouded my eyes, mixing with the rain.

Before the officer could answer, someone started speaking over his radio.

"Victims were DOA, standby!"

My chest tightened and I felt like I was about to pass out.

"Ma'am," the officer said.

Everything grew blurry as my knees buckled. The cop caught me right before I fell, and I let out a gut-wrenching scream.

To Be Continued...